"I want something from you, Beau.

"I've been planning this for months, though I hadn't really given a lot of thought to how exactly I would do it..." Lily continued. "But when you showed up, and fit every one of my criteria, I couldn't ignore..."

"Criteria? What criteria?" Beau frowned.

"Experienced, available and temporary."

"Available for what?"

"Sex, of course," Lily said simply.

Beau's jaw dropped. "E-excuse me?"

She looked at him as if he were a backward child. "I came here tonight because I decided that the only way I'm ever going to have the kind of sexual experience I want is with a man of the world."

"But you don't know me," he protested, shaking his head.

Lily smiled as if everything made perfect sense. "That's what makes you the ideal man."

Dear Reader,

The age-old question of why a woman would choose a bad boy over a nice guy has always had a pretty obvious answer, as far as I'm concerned. Let's face it. Bad boys are just more fun. Lily Matthews, my heroine in *Southern Comforts*, would agree. In fact, she's on a quest to find a bad boy of her very own. So when reckless Beau Stuart rolls into town, he doesn't stand a chance....

Beau has met a lot of women in his time, but he's never come across one like Lily. When she offers him the opportunity for a hot and heavy, no-strings affair, he knows he'd be a fool to turn her down. And Beau's no fool—certainly not for love. But while he thinks he's got the situation, and Lily, under control, he's losing his edge...and his heart.

So, what does it take to tame a bad boy? I'm not sure you can. But the important question is, do you want to? I think Lily found her answer, and I know she found her man. I hope you enjoy their special love story.

Sincerely,

Sandy Steen

SOUTHERN COMFORTS
Sandy Steen

HARLEQUIN®

TORONTO • NEW YORK • LONDON
AMSTERDAM • PARIS • SYDNEY • HAMBURG
STOCKHOLM • ATHENS • TOKYO • MILAN • MADRID
PRAGUE • WARSAW • BUDAPEST • AUCKLAND

For my friend, June Harvey.

For all the victims of breast cancer, and especially for the survivors and their families who have battled so bravely and give us the strength to fight on.

ISBN 0-373-25873-9

SOUTHERN COMFORTS

Copyright © 2000 by Sandy Steen.

1

THE WOMAN CAUGHT HIS EYE the minute she strolled out of the library, heading for the small park across the street. But at that moment if someone had asked Beau Stuart, he couldn't have said why. Drop-dead gorgeous she wasn't. No short skirt. No model's figure. And certainly no designer clothes; just a plain brown dress. Maybe it was the way the sunlight highlighted her chestnut-colored hair, held at her nape with a nondescript barrette. Even from a distance, or more accurately from experience, he could tell it was thick. He liked women with long, thick hair. Something to run his fingers through or hold on to when passion ran high. Or maybe it was the way she walked that had snagged his attention—a walk that was all grace and glide, that produced the sexiest, most enticing little sway he had admired in a long time. Yeah, it had to be the sway. To begin with, she was walking away from him at an angle so he couldn't fully see her face. And for another, he was a fan of the feminine derriere. Hell, he was a connoisseur. This woman might not be the type that usually drew his attention, but she had a world-class fanny and walk to match. He was disappointed when she sat down on a park bench, put on her glasses and opened a book, but not enough to look away. He was curious why a woman with such an eye-catching walk didn't dress with a little more flair. He couldn't remember when he'd seen a woman less conscientious about her appearance. Her dress appeared neat and clean, but definitely outdated, particularly for someone young. Consequences of living in a small town, he suspected, or maybe her income was limited. The phrase "poor but proud" came to mind—a phrase he'd heard his mother use more times that he cared to remember. Beau frowned. He didn't even know the lady in brown, but he didn't like to think of her being poor, particularly in this town. He sure as hell knew what that felt like. Old memories surfaced, but he shut them out before they had a chance to ruin his mood. He trained his thoughts on the lady in brown.

An appropriate moniker, he thought, summing her up as not just ordinary, but monochromatic brown. Brown hair—okay, he'd give her the highlights. Brown dress trimmed in beige—nice fit. In fact, she had a better than nice figure from what he saw as she had strolled to the park. Beige low-heel pumps—an injustice considering her deliciously long legs. He wouldn't be surprised to discover she had brown eyes behind those glasses. Soft brown, like a doe's. He wished she'd lift her head, glance his way. Again, he wasn't sure why. She was as far from the kind of woman that usually interested him as the North Pole from the South. He liked his women sassy, sexy and savvy. This one looked like a home-grown Pollyanna. Trouble, as far as he was concerned, because they were usually looking for the 3/2/2 lifestyle. Three bedrooms, two baths, two-car garage. Those numbers added up to only one thing—commitment. Trite, but true. He'd get around to a family one of these days, but he wasn't ready now. So, he'd become a master mathematician of sorts. He could spot a 3/2/2 woman from a half mile and avoided her at all cost. Pollyanna had that look, but just around the edges. Still, there was something very compelling about her, something...

"Don't even think about it."

Beau turned to find T. J. Howard—his best friend and, for Beau's money, the best damned business attorney on the East Coast—standing at the bottom of the steps leading into the First National Bank of Rosemont. "Think about what?"

"I saw you watching the sweet young thing sitting in the park. And I'm telling you, Beau, forget her. She's not your type."

Beau had been bucking the system for so much of his life, rising to the bait of a challenge, even a nibble from a good friend brought out the rebel in him. "They say variety is the spice of life. Maybe I should broaden my horizons."

"Your horizons get any broader and one of these days I'll end up representing you in a paternity suit."

Beau cut his eye to his friend. "That'll never happen."

"Besides, you mess with that one and the whole town will be down on you so fast you won't know what hit you."

"They're already down on me."

T.J. winced. "Don't I know it. Mind telling me why you even bother to hang around here? I mean, it's not like you need the money. Your import business is flourishing. So's the hockey team and computer business. You're already a millionaire several times over."

"Don't try to sidetrack me. Who is she?"

"Local girl. Say, listen, you need to sign some documents in connection with the estate taxes and—"

"You might as well tell me who she is because I'll find out sooner or later. Probably sooner."

"Beau—"

"C'mon, T.J."

Knowing it was useless to protest further, T.J. sighed. "Her ancestor, Tobias Jackson, practically founded the town. Some far distant relative of Stonewall Jackson. "

"Tobias Jackson. I remember that name from when I was a kid. They grew tobacco, and raised horses, I think."

"Yeah. Old Civil War family. Had money once,

but what they didn't lose during the Depression, the ne'er-do-well sons either invested badly or gambled away. Dead broke now. In fact, shortly before you were born, Rowland Stuart bought most of what had once been Jackson holdings, including the house."

"Great. Dear old dad bought the ole plantation out from under Little Nell over there. That certainly insures me a warm welcome."

"Beau, I said she wasn't your type and I meant it. The Matthews may have fallen on hard times, but they're considered true Southern gentry. Real magnolias and mint julep stuff."

"Thought you said their name was Jackson."

"Her mother's maiden name. The father was John Matthews."

"Was?"

"He took off with another woman, leaving his wife almost an invalid. She does old-fashioned handwork to sell in a few of Richmond's specialty shops, and Lily is the town librarian."

"Lily?"

"That's Little Nell's name, Lily Matthews."

Beau's grin turned sly. "You know, in all my...travels, shall we say, I don't think I've ever dated a librarian."

"Now, Beau, I know you can't resist a challenge, and that gleam in your eyes is nothing short of dangerous, but don't you think you've got enough on your plate without intentionally looking for trouble?

I thought you were in a hurry to finalize everything."

"Trouble? It's the last thing on my mind." A true statement if ever there was one, considering Lily Matthews's enticing sway was uppermost in his thoughts. "Anyway," he said, in a slow, deep drawl that affected most women like catnip affected cats, "you know I never hurry where women are concerned."

"If that was meant to reassure me, it needs work."

Beau didn't have to ask how his attorney knew so much about Little Nell and her family background. T.J. was the most thorough man he'd ever met, a quality that had saved Beau millions of dollars and much anxiety over the years. And he was willing to bet there was a thick file on T.J.'s desk with lots more information on Lily Matthews and probably ninety percent of the rest of the Rosemont population. Strange, but he didn't remember her, and they must have gone to school together, unless, of course, she was a lot younger. Even if he had known her as a child, it's no wonder he didn't remember her now. He'd tried hard to forget everything about this town. Now, here he was, right back where he started.

"I'm a pariah to the whole damned town anyway and nothing I do or say is going to change that. So, I might as well have some fun. Like you said, I can't resist a challenge. And I'll bet my Hummer, Lily the librarian hasn't had a lot of excitement in her life. Am I right?"

When T.J. groaned, Beau said, "Thought so," and slapped him on the back. "Relax, I promise I won't do anything illegal or outrageously expensive."

"You left out immoral."

Beau smiled, then laughed out loud when T.J. shook his head and lifted his gaze heavenward. "Life's too short to ignore the possibilities," Beau said, looking at Lily Matthews, her back ramrod straight, her posture perfect as she read. Even the way she held her book was precise. So prim and proper. Hell, he'd bet his Hummer she was probably still a virgin. Now, that was intriguing. "Besides," he told T.J. as he headed in the direction of the park, "some fantastic things come in plain brown wrappers."

LILY TRIED TO CONCENTRATE on the book of poetry and couldn't. All she could think about was the gossip. When it came to passing along information Ma Bell had nothing on the Rosemont grapevine, and at the moment it was humming at the speed of light. And all about one man.

Beauregard Mosby Stuart.

Lily closed the book, perched her glasses atop her head and sighed. She'd heard the whispers and speculation tinged with disdain. They said he was a hellion. A rebel with a cause. They said he'd been noth-

ing but a troublemaker the first ten years of his life
when he'd lived in Rosemont and he'd only gotten
worse.

They also said he was handsome as sin and
smooth-talking enough to convince the devil into going to church.

Every time Lily thought about her one brief
glimpse of Beau Stuart, she had to agree that if he
was as smooth-talking as he was good-looking she
wouldn't be surprised to see Lucifer himself singing
psalms next Sunday. And every time she thought
about the whispered rumors of his prowess with
women, her heart beat a little faster. Actually a lot
faster. Wouldn't her mother and Aunt Pauline be
shocked to know such thoughts were racing around
her brain. Lily was a little shocked herself, but not
enough to stop thinking about the tall, sexy stranger
who had practically turned the little Virginia town
upside down since his arrival three days ago. The
whole town was talking of nothing else and secretly
she admitted she wanted a closer look at this real life
hell-raiser. To see for herself if Beau Stuart was as
dashing, dangerous and rebellious as everyone
claimed. She was simply aching to find out just how
much was fact and how much was fiction. Not that
she'd had any real experience with dashing and dangerous. But fiction was a different story. There, she
was in her element. She'd learned the meaning of
dashing and dangerous from a long list of males,

everyone from James Bond to Zorro. Lily had only gotten a glimpse of Beau Stuart, but it was enough to pique her interest, stir her imagination and whet an appetite she hoped to cultivate.

He was from another world as far as she was concerned, like one of the characters she'd read about all her life. A world of excitement, glamour, exotic places and events. A world filled with intelligent people and conversations a thousand times more scintillating than the fact that Miss Annabelle McCormick, retired schoolteacher, took high tea in Richmond every Wednesday afternoon and always returned a little high herself. One of the most exciting aspects of Beau Stuart was his reputation with women. Some of it was undoubtedly embellished because it made good copy, but there had been too many women and too much copy for a great deal of it not to be true. There was scarcely a month that passed without his picture appearing in the newspaper, taken at a society function, hockey game or benefit, and he was always with a beautiful woman. Sometimes more than one. And even though he'd been born in Rosemont, and spent some of his young years there, Lily doubted Beau Stuart gave a thought to the kind of existence that passed for a life in his little hometown. Everything about him looked polished and sophisticated, beginning with the huge and very attention-getting vehicle she'd seen him in that first day. Most people in town had only seen a

Humby in the movies so, even if someone else had been driving, they would have stared. Since it was Beau Stuart, they gawked. And Lily had to admit she'd gawked right along with them.

That was the day Rowland Stuart's will had been read, stunning the town with the news that everything had been left to Beau instead of Rebecca Stuart, widow to Rowland's oldest son, Rowland Jr., his only legitimate son.

Old man Stuart was one of the wealthiest men in the county. In fact, he had vast real estate holdings, including the original land and grand plantation house he called home. And last, but certainly not least, he owned the computer chip factory that employed over sixty percent of the Rosemont work force. Now it all belonged to Beau. To a man that had been denied his father's name but had taken it anyway. To a man who had been shunned by most of the town's people as a boy. He and his mother. Was it any wonder Beau had never returned until now? It would certainly be understandable if he bore no love in his heart for Rosemont or its citizens. Lily didn't have to reach far to imagine what he must have gone through as a child. Shame and anger weren't foreign emotions, although she had learned to hold her feelings inside and her head high. In a way Beau was lucky. He got away. Lily had never had that option. She might want to turn her back on Rosemont, and had thought of it often enough, but she could never turn her back on her mother.

So, she was familiar with the ever-humming grapevine. But now, woven among all the whispers was a thread of fear. What would be Beau Stuart's attitude toward the town after all these years? What if he decided to take back a little of his own for the way he and his mother had been treated? He practically held Rosemont's economy in his hands and no one knew what he intended to do with it, but most assumed the worst. Lily frowned. She didn't like the way everyone had judged Beau based on his past. She knew what that felt like. Perhaps that's why she now viewed the day Beau Stuart decided to stay in Rosemont until the estate was settled as a gift from...fate? If she had run an ad in the Rosemont Register that read: Wanted, One Sexy, Smooth-talking Scoundrel, she couldn't have done any better. It had to be fate. How else could she account for the fact that after months of a mental tug-of-war with herself she'd made the life-changing decision not to die a virgin and, voilà...along came Beau Stuart?

If ever there was a perfect man to relieve her of that particular burden, he was it. So what if the winds of chance had swept Beau into town and across her path? So what if it had been wish fulfillment, or a voodoo spell complete with live chickens? What difference did it make? He was exactly what she was looking for. Experienced, available and temporary.

The temporary part was very important because she didn't intend to carry on a long-term affair. Nor did she want to have her heart broken. She suspected the rumors about Beau leaving a trail of broken hearts behind him at least a mile wide was more truth than rumor. He probably kept two or three women on a string at the same time. A scoundrel of the highest order... In short, exactly the kind of man she needed.

Lily wasn't even sure when the idea of deliberately seeking out a lover had first come to her, and for a while she thought she must be losing her mind to even think of such a drastic step. But as the years passed, her hopes of ever meeting Mr. Right had faded. It had become clear that if ever her knight on a white horse *had* been headed in her direction, he'd taken the wrong off-ramp on the superhighway of romance. Now, finding a lover was the challenge. There certainly were no viable candidates in Rosemont, not that she would have seriously considered a local man because of the risk of discovery. In fact, the only part of the plan that truly gave her cause for concern was that she would have to keep it a secret from the one person whose opinion and counsel she valued most. Her mother. Everything Lily had been taught her entire life was based on honesty and compassion. In this case the most compassionate thing to do was make sure her mother never found out what she intended to do.

Not because she thought her mother wouldn't understand, but because, if her actions ever came to light, she wasn't sure Amelia Matthews could survive another scandal. The first one, over twenty years ago, had left her almost an invalid. The doctors said she had a weak heart, but over the years Lily had come to believe it was a broken heart. When John Matthews abandoned his sweet young wife and four-year-old daughter for a woman three years his senior and rumored to have once been a madam in Atlanta, the gossip, speculation and outright lies were too painful to bear. For a man to choose that kind of woman over one of class and good breeding, the man was either crazy or... It was the "or" that had haunted her mother for almost twenty years, and her gentle spirit never quite recovered.

The thought that she might cause her mother any more pain had been the primary reason she hadn't taken this impetuous step before now. Of course, a fling with any man in Rosemont was out of the question, but even one from nearby Richmond was a risk. Too many people in this county were related. Too many idle tongues. The man she chose had to be from out of town, someone that didn't care about what the town thought or said about him.

That was the most important reason Beau Stuart was perfect for her plan. He had no interest in talking to the Rosemont citizenry and they certainly had no desire to speak to him.

Lily glanced at her watch. "Oh, now I'm late." She tucked the book beneath her arm, gathered up the remains of her sack lunch and headed for the library. Hurrying along, she didn't see the man approaching the door at the same time and nearly collided with him. Her hand all but knocked his away as they reached for the door handle at the same time. "I'm so sorry. Please, excuse..." She glanced up and her jaw dropped.

It was him! Beau Stuart. Standing next to her. Close enough to touch.

Lily knew she was staring, knew she still had her hand outstretched, but couldn't look away or move. If she'd thought him handsome at a distance he was devastating at close range. But she would never again choose a word as ordinary as handsome to describe Beau Stuart. Square jaw, blue eyes, dark, wavy hair—all the elements of rugged good looks, but the way they were arranged was nothing short of breathtaking. Yes, that was the sensation. As if all the air had suddenly left her lungs. But it didn't stop there. There was something primitive, something so powerfully male about him. Call it chemistry or just sex appeal. Whatever you called it, he had it. Like an aura that practically shimmered from his body like heat shimmering from the pavement at noon on an August day. It engulfed, infused and invaded. At least that's what was happening to her. The prospect of Beau as her designated lover suddenly took on a whole new dimension of reality. The reality of her response.

It had to be lust. Pure sexual attraction. Not that she could name it from experience, but it couldn't be anything else. And the power was overwhelming. She actually felt flushed and a little dizzy.

"Allow me."

"W-what?"

He smiled and she was positive her heart actually skipped a beat. "Allow me to get the door," he said, his smooth, deep voice only adding to the impact of his maleness rushing toward her like storm waves across the sea.

Lily drew her hand back. "Yes, uh... Yes, thank... you." It was the first time in her life that she could actually admit to herself that she was glad the gossip was true.

Once inside the library she felt better, the familiar surroundings bringing instant stability. It also helped that she was able to take several steps away from Beau Stuart. Even so, she took a deep breath before turning to face him. And she needed it, because he was just standing there looking at her.

"Can I help you?" she asked in her best librarian-in-charge voice, and hoped he didn't notice the quiver.

Beau gave her a slow once-over. Yeah, she could

help him. Help him off with his clothes and into a bed. What the hell had he been thinking to dub this woman dull brown? His thoughts of "better than nice" figure might just be the understatement of the century. Make that the millennium. The full-on front view of Little Nell was anything but girlish. He hadn't seen a woman with such a lush, ripe body in a long time, and his own responded predictably. No skin and bones here. No siree. This was curves and soft flesh in just the right amounts and in exactly the right places. She had the kind of body that would have made Botticelli drool. Hell, it was making *him* drool. And to top it off, she'd had the most charming look of surprised awareness on her face when she'd glanced up. He'd spent so much time with sophisticated females he'd almost forgotten what innocence looked like. It looked great on her. A little at odds with her built-for-the-bedroom body, but the combination had real potential. He liked that sort of duality, especially in bed.

"Yes," he finally managed to answer.

She licked her lips and tilted her head just the slightest bit to her right and heat shot straight to his groin. When he didn't elaborate, she cleared her throat, squared her shoulders and said, "Sir?"

If she was going to draw attention to herself like that, a man couldn't be held responsible for lustful thoughts or urges, he decided, struggling to peel his eyes away from her ample chest. But then he caught the heightened color in her cheeks and saw the demure veneer settle back into place. The wide-eyed innocence had been checked, and prim and proper were back.

"Did you have a particular author or subject in mind?"

She might be able to fool the small town men with that distancing trick, but prim and proper was his specialty. Oh, this was going to be much more fun than he'd thought. He gave her a slow, melting smile and was gratified to see that her eyes sparkled even if her demeanor stayed in place. "Actually, Ms...."

"Lily Matthews. I'm the librarian."

"Well, Ms. Matthews, I used to live around here and—"

"Yes, I know, Mr. Stuart."

That surprised him. Not that she would know, but that she would say it right out like that. Either she was the exception to the rule, or the citizens of Rosemont had gotten a lot more honest since he left. "Call me Beau." He offered his hand.

Lily had intended a quick, nonpersonal shake, but it wasn't in the cards. If she hadn't known she was awake, standing in the library in broad daylight, she might have thought she'd fallen asleep reading a passage from one of her favorite romance authors, because the instant their hands touched she felt something that could only be described as a tingle. And heat. Lots of heat.

"Nice to meet you, Lily."

"And you." She couldn't bring herself to say his name for fear it might come out all breathy and girlish. She hated that kind of immature behavior some women thought was a necessary component in their bag of feminine tricks.

"Since you know who I am, no sense pretending I'm lost or just looking to check out a copy of Grisham's latest."

"You don't want a book?"

The corner of his mouth lifted ever so slightly into a decidedly wicked grin. "No, ma'am, I don't."

"So why did you come in?"

"I followed you."

"Pardon me?"

"I said, I followed you."

"Why?" The blunt question was out before she realized she'd spoken. Why didn't she learn to keep her mouth closed? This sort of speaking before thinking had always gotten her in trouble. "Excuse me. That was rude and I—"

"You're a lovely woman. I'm a healthy, reasonably attractive man, so I let nature take the lead and I followed. That process has worked pretty well for several thousand years, so I see no need to fix what ain't broke."

"You mean you came in here just to...to..."

"Meet you, then ask you out. Would you have dinner with me?"

"Me?"

"Is there an echo in this library? Yes, you, Ms. Lily Matthews." Suddenly he frowned. "It's not Mrs., is it? You're not married or engaged, or anything?"

"No." On second thought, this had to be a dream.

He sighed. "That's a relief. Had me worried for a minute, because I sure would like to take you to dinner tonight." He stepped closer, lowered his voice. "And please don't disappoint me by telling me you already have plans."

Oh, he should bottle that charm, she thought. He could go from millionaire to trillionaire overnight. "Well, I—"

"We'll go someplace real nice where they have great food, soft lights, maybe even some music. I always think music enhances the flavor no matter what the food, don't you?" He stopped when he saw the strange look in her eyes and the faintest suggestion of a frown. "Why so puzzled? Have I said something wrong?"

"No, it's just..."

"Just what?"

"Well, to be frank, Mr.—"

"By all means, and the name's Beau."

"All right, Beau. Well, to be frank we don't know each other and—"

"We'll get acquainted over a thick steak. Or something lighter if you're not a meat-eater."

"Steak is fine, but..." How could she tell him that

she'd been rehearsing what to say to him, how to get him to invite her out, and he'd taken her so completely by surprise she was flabbergasted? "I—I... You're not supposed to—"

"Oh." The grin vanished. "I get it," he said, stepping back. "My reputation precedes me, is that it? Once a bad seed, always a bad seed. I didn't realize my horns were showing."

She'd known Beau Stuart all of five minutes, and there was no question he was a smooth-talker, but there wasn't enough smoothness in the world to hide pain. It was there in his eyes and she suspected it was an old and deep wound. Third-degree rejection.

"You know, Lily, it's damned hard for a man to redeem himself if nobody ever gives him a second chance. I liked the look of you right off. And when we started to talk I liked you even more for your candor, but I suppose I can't expect you to go against—"

"No, that has nothing to do with it." When he looked dubious she added, "Really." A half lie at best and she probably would have continued, giving him a socially acceptable excuse if she hadn't seen the pain in his eyes. If she hadn't recognized it. Identified with it. Now she could only match his honesty. "I know a lot of people in town have judged you based on the past, but please believe me, I'm not one of them. It's just that I...I can't imagine why you would want to take me to dinner."

"Are you serious?"

"Are you?"

"As judgment day." He doubted there was a coy bone in her body, but she wasn't making this easy. But then, he reminded himself, nothing worthwhile ever is. Of course, he wasn't going to ravish her at the first opportunity. He planned to save that until they got to know each other better. Like the second date. "To begin with, you're smart. Gotta be if you're the librarian, right? And second..." The grin was back. "Well, let's face it." His gaze swept her from head to toe and back again. "From those long, gorgeous legs to those big brown eyes, you're one terrific piece of eye candy."

"Eye candy?"

"Definitely." When he didn't see comprehension in her eyes, he said flat out. "Darlin', you're just plain great to look at."

"Oh." Now it was her turn to step back. "Oh... thank you."

"Strictly my pleasure. Now, how about tonight?"

"Tonight." The way he said pleasure, slow as molasses and soft as a summer night, made her want to sigh.

"Yeah. You, me, a juicy steak, soft lights and music. What time shall I pick you up?"

"Pick me up." Everything sounded so wonderful the way he said it. Mercy, but the man was mesmerizing.

"Gotta do something about that echo, Miss Lily."

"Oh." Reluctantly she came back to reality. And reality meant secrecy. "Oh, yes. Well, uh..."

"Seven okay with you?"

"Yes, but I'm not always out of here right at five o'clock, so...why don't I just meet you at your house? How would that be? Or, I could meet you at whatever restaurant you select."

For a second Beau was startled at her unexpected offer, then it all made sense. She meant after dark. Less chance of being seen that way. It stung a little, but he couldn't blame her. In fact he gave her credit. The lady knew how to look out for herself.

"Whatever works for you, works for me."

"I'm, uh...sometimes I get tied up and have to stay a few minutes after closing."

"You said that."

"Oh, did I?"

"You're not thinking about backing out are you, Miss Lily?" He closed the distance between them. "'Cause that would break my heart."

"I...I...no, I'm not backing out."

Beau reached out, picked up a thick curl lying close to her throat. Gazing into her eyes, he toyed with the strands for a second, then slowly, as if nothing else in the world could have been more important, he returned it to its resting place.

"Glad to hear it." He glanced around, noticed half the people in the library were watching them, then looked back at her. "You know, I'd halfway decided to leave town today and let my attorney deal with the business details, but I've changed my mind. Or, maybe I should say, meeting a certain librarian changed it for me."

Smiling, Beau turned to leave, but stopped at the door. "Remember, I'm counting on you not to break my heart." Then he was gone.

Lily stared at the empty doorway, knowing without a doubt that the gossip was true. The proverbial "they" were right. He was handsome as sin, and as for being a smooth-talker... Well, someone should tell the parson they'd better heat-proof the front pew come Sunday.

AS BEAU WALKED back to his car the thought crossed his mind that she might truly be as innocent as she looked. It was also possible she was too good to be true. She could be using his invitation to get information he was certain ninety-nine percent of the townspeople wanted. Namely, did he intend to sell the microchip factory? He didn't know any more about Lily Matthews than what T.J. had told him, but his instincts insisted she was trustworthy. He'd made a lot of money following his instincts, particularly with hostile takeovers. In and out of the boardroom. Beau smiled. So, if the librarian with the built-for-the-bedroom body wanted answers she would go home disappointed. On the other hand, if she wanted a little hands-on, up close and personal Southern comfort, he would be more than happy to oblige.

2

THE HOUSE LILY SHARED with her mother was only a few blocks from the library and she always walked, weather permitting. It gave her time to put her day in perspective. And today of all days she needed perspective.

She'd done it!

She'd taken the first step. She couldn't believe she'd actually done it. And while part of her was stunned at her audacity, she had to admit it had been much easier than she'd expected. Of course, Beau had made it easy.

Now all she had to do was go through with her plan.

Lily stopped walking. For the first time she realized that making her decision and finding the right man was the total of her grand plan. She'd never really taken the time to flesh out the details, so to speak. Little things, like would they go to a motel or his house? Should she take the sleek black nightgown she'd bought on a whim then secretly stowed away under her wool sweaters? Would they do it before or after dinner? And just how did she intend to tell him what she wanted from him? *Could I please have another helping of salad? And by the way, I'd also like to have sex with you.*

Suddenly it all sounded so ridiculous. And impossible. And she panicked.

In the throes of a full-blown panic attack she started walking again, only faster. Oh God, what had she done? Whatever made her think she could go through with this walk on the wild side? It was totally out of character. Totally out of the question.

She had to cancel, and that's all there was to it. She would just call Beau and tell him...what? That she had a headache. That she remembered a previous engagement. Or that she was temporarily insane...

Lily stopped walking and forced herself to take several deep breaths. No, what she was doing *now* was insane.

That phone call to him would relegate her to living vicariously through the pages of her books again, dreaming of a man that would never appear.

But he had appeared. Almost like magic.

Not magic. In her mind, magic and romance were almost synonymous and she certainly didn't want romance mixed up in this. Besides, at twenty-five she was too levelheaded to believe in magic, even if the man of her dreams had appeared just when she despaired of that ever happening. Coincidence, maybe. Pure chance, probably. But not magic. The same logic that had prompted her to say yes to his invitation in the first place still held. And she could do this. Had to do this—for herself. She had to forget, or at least set aside all the "dos and don'ts" regarding respectable behavior that she'd abided by all her life. She had to focus on her goal.

"Focus, Lily. Focus," she whispered as she came up the walk and onto the front porch of her home. From inside she heard her Aunt Pauline's tinny and incessant voice, probably delivering the latest gossip to her mother. Lily took a few more deep breaths and went inside.

"Well, there you are." Pauline Jackson, widow to the last male Jackson in the county, drew herself up to her full five feet three inches. "You had your mother worried sick."

Amelia Matthews shot her sister-in-law an exasperated look. "I wasn't any such thing. I know Lily can't always walk out of the library right at five."

"Hello, Aunt Pauline. Sorry, last minute returns," Lily said, giving her mother a kiss on the cheek. "Wouldn't you know, the one day I'm in a hurry."

"Hurry?" Pauline asked. "Hurry for what?"

"Lily called me a little while ago to tell me she's meeting that friend of hers, Connie, the one that works at the historical society in Richmond. They're going to dinner, then an outdoor concert."

"Why, you never mentioned anything to me about Lily going out."

"Pauline, you've only been here fifteen minutes

and you've been talking the whole time. When would I have told you?"

"Well, just the same, if I'm expected to keep an eye on you whenever Lily goes *traipsing* off, I need some advance notice."

"No need to concern yourself. Mrs. McCreary from across the street is coming over to keep me company. She has a new coverlet pattern she's been dying to show me."

"Well, if you two will excuse me I have to jump in the shower—" she winked at her mother "—before I go *traipsing* off." Then she made a strategic retreat before her aunt could take up her favorite role of grand inquisitor. She had no doubt her mother was receiving the requisite twenty questions and hoped she had given her just enough information to satisfy Aunt Pauline, or anyone else for that matter. Selecting her friend, Connie, as an alibi was easy and logical. They usually went to a movie or dinner at least once a month, so her mother would accept their going out without question. She had called Connie before she called her mother to be sure there were no slipups. The outdoor concert, too, was logical. There actually was a concert, but it was classical music and she doubted few people in Rosemont knew about the event, much less planned to attend. Her only real concern was that someone might recognize her car at his place, but she counted on the animosity toward Beau to aid in her efforts at secrecy. So far, the townspeople had stayed away from the Stuart mansion in droves. She had checked and double-checked her story, made sure all loose ends were tied and prayed nothing went wrong. Her story was elaborate, and probably unnecessary for this evening, despite her earlier fears of what to say and how to say it. She didn't really expect anything to happen tonight. After all, a woman doesn't just go to a man's house, ask him to be her lover and expect him to say yes then drag her off to the bedroom. Still, this was too important to leave anything to chance.

When she'd made her decision to end her twenty-four years of chastity, Lily confronted realities she couldn't avoid. Unwanted pregnancy was part of that reality. She'd started taking birth control pills almost three weeks ago, but her doctor had warned her some women require a full twenty-eight to thirty-day cycle before they were fully protected. He strongly advised using condoms as well. Clutching the hope of meeting Beau, she'd made a discreet trip into a Richmond drugstore yesterday. A box of twelve condoms was safely tucked into a folded pair of socks and hidden inside her chest of drawers. She was prepared, in so much as she could prepare for something she personally knew nothing about.

Thirty minutes later, freshly bathed and shampooed, Lily stood staring at the only dress suitable for her date with Beau Stuart. Like the black nightgown, she'd bought the dress but never worn it. Not

that it was wildly daring. Well, maybe it was for her.
But she had seen the slip-dress with matching
cropped cardigan in a catalog and ordered it by
phone before she could change her mind. Even so,
she'd almost returned it unopened when it was delivered. But she made the mistake of opening the
package and, once she'd held the rust-colored silk in
her hands, she knew she couldn't send it back. She
was so thrilled with the dress she even ordered new,
and decidedly sexy, underwear to go with the outfit,
plus a pair of shoes. All of it was way over her
budget, but if she was going to go, she might as well
go all the way. Now, as she slipped the dress over
her head and it settled around her body, she was
glad that she had. The silk was soft, flowing and she
felt a little naughty just thinking of how it moved
against her skin. Good, a little naughty was exactly
what was called for tonight, she thought, reaching
for her jewelry box. A simple gold bracelet and
dainty gold earrings for finishing touches. A quick
glance in her full-length mirror and...Lily did a double take.

"Wow," she whispered, reaching for her glasses
just to make sure of what she was seeing.

Lily knew she wasn't exactly plain and she'd been
blessed with a good figure, but until now she'd
never thought of herself as sexy. But in this dress,
with her hair cascading over her shoulders and just a
hint of makeup, she was damned attractive, if she

did say so herself. It was like seeing a beautiful twin for the first time. Shocking, but exciting. Of course, Beau might not be impressed. He was used to women much more beautiful and sophisticated. One little country girl in a new dress was hardly...

"Stop that!" Lily hissed, forcing the negative thoughts aside. "Remember your goal." With that, she made a mental note to remember to ditch her glasses before she got to his house, and started to leave. But she stopped, remembering the box of condoms.

"Like something will really happen," she said. But a small voice in her head urged caution. Better safe than sorry. She walked to the chest, opened the drawer and collected two foil-wrapped packets from their hiding place. Then she gathered all of her courage, and off she went.

As BEAU CAME DOWN the wide staircase to the foyer of the Stuart mansion he glanced into the dining room with its ornate crystal chandelier and a table that would seat at least twelve, and congratulated himself on his decision to have dinner served in the more intimate setting. Besides, he thought Lily would think the library was a nice, personal touch and he was out to score all the points he could. Even though the spring night wasn't chilly he'd had a fire lit and enough candles placed around the room to give the oak paneled walls and bookshelves warmth and welcome. Fresh flowers had been placed in the entryway and on the table. He didn't know what it was about fresh flowers in a man's home, but women always seemed to be impressed. He'd seen them go all soft and dewy over something as simple as a vase of gladiolas. Far be it from him to attempt to decipher the complex feminine mind, but he certainly wasn't above using it to his advantage.

Tonight there was an arrangement of some sort of lilies, another touch he hoped she noticed, in the entryway and a small nosegay of violets on the table. He'd thought about orchids, but decided they were overkill. And when the woman at the florist shop had suggested violets they seemed a perfect fit. The table was set, the wine was chilled and he'd polished his best manners. Now all he needed—the doorbell chimed and he smiled at the timing—was his companion.

Armed with his most charming smile, Beau opened the door. "Good eve—" he'd intended to add a gallant bow, but one look at her and the plan flew right out of his head "—ning." For a second he wasn't sure she was the same woman he'd met that afternoon. Except for her eyeglasses, the transformation was stunning. Her complexion was breathtaking, his gaze glided over its smooth milkiness, then settled on her mouth. Why hadn't he noticed how lush and full her lips were? And he couldn't take his eyes off her hair, tumbling gloriously around her shoulders. She reminded him of an exotic gypsy girl in a painting he'd once admired.

"Lily?" She didn't answer immediately and for a second she looked as if she intended to turn and run. "Won't you, uh, come in?"

"What? Oh, yes. Thank you." Lily stepped over the threshold.

"Here, let me help you," he offered, as she struggled with her coat.

"Thanks."

He hung the coat on an antique hall tree then turned back and froze.

If his first glimpse of her hit him like a tidal wave, this one was a tsunami. Stunning didn't even begin to cover the way she looked. Her dress had to be silk the way it clung to—make that caressed—her body. The color might still have been in the brown family but there was damn sure nothing plain about it. The shade of deep rust caught the light in all the right places, outlining her figure. From where he stood, she was wearing the perfect dress for their date: short, sexy and easy to remove. This was too good to be true. He had to stop staring or he was going to make a fool of himself.

The battalion of butterflies marching cadence in the pit of Lily's stomach halted at the look of total surprise on Beau's face. In that moment she knew her blown budget and all her anxieties were worth it.

"That's, uh..." Beau recovered just in time to stop

himself from drooling. "That's some dress." Not to mention the body beneath it.

"You like it?"

"Oh, yeah." Grinning, he walked right up to her, so close she could hardly breathe. "Why, Miss Jones," he reached out and removed her glasses, "you're beautiful."

Lily's hands flew to her face. "Oh, I forgot I even... I only need them to read, or...at night, and—"

"Well, I must admit they didn't do much for the dress. You, on the other hand—" he lifted her hand and kissed it "—do."

"Thank...thank you." The spot where his mouth touched her skin felt hot and tingly. Pleasantly so. In fact, the sensations spread, almost as if they had penetrated her skin and entered her bloodstream. Heady, she thought. Deliciously intoxicating. Then she looked into his eyes. Her life was filled with words, but for the first time she knew the real meaning of words like enthralled, mesmerized. His eyes weren't just blue, but a hundred shades of blue with a flame flickering in their depths. Hot, like his lips. Intensely sensual. Suddenly she understood and sympathized with the moth fatally attracted to the enticing flame. Reluctantly she reclaimed her hand. She didn't want to fling herself at the man's feet and beg him to make love to her. Well, that wasn't quite true. But she reminded herself that he was a man of the world. If she fell all over him now, it might turn him off and there would go her chance.

"Do we, uh, have reservations?"

"Reservations?"

"Yes. You know, at a restaurant."

Beau stepped away. A wise move since the move he wanted to make was to kiss her until neither of them could breathe. Maybe later. For now, he had to deal with making sure she didn't bolt when he told her they weren't going out. "Are you hungry?"

Oh, he had no idea. "Starving, actually."

Beau frowned.

"Something wrong," she asked. "Couldn't you get reservations at a restaurant?"

"I'm not sure how to say this... In fact, I've probably presumed way too much, but..."

"But what?"

"Let me show you something." He took her hand and led her to two double wooden doors. "Now, if I've stepped over the line here, I'll get your coat and we'll be outta here in two shakes of a lamb's tail."

"I don't understand."

"I thought it might be nice if we had dinner here." He opened both doors to reveal the intimate setting. "Now, before you say no—"

"I wouldn't dream of it. In fact, I think it's a wonderful idea." Lily smiled sweetly then walked into the room.

Beau had been prepared to turn up the charm a

notch or two, even knew exactly the approach he intended to take to convince her to stay, but she'd surrendered without him firing a shot.

"Well, great. I'm...relieved. I was afraid you might get the wrong idea and be offended."

"When you've obviously gone to so much trouble, that's not offensive. Quite the contrary." Still smiling, she gazed around the room. "It's perfect."

He must be dreaming. That was it. Had to be. Any minute now he was going to wake up and discover he'd been having one helluva dream.

Then Lily slipped off her little cardigan, walked to the fireplace and turned to face him. The combination of candlelight and firelight on her skin, her hair, the way it cast shadows and highlights on her body, told him nothing could be more real. He was hard before he could draw a full breath.

Slowly he walked to the bar set up next to the table. "Would you like a glass of wine?"

"I think so."

"Red or white?"

"You choose."

He was halfway through filling her glass with zinfandel when she added, "I've never had wine so I'll trust your judgment."

He stopped pouring. "Never?"

"No. I've read about it, of course. I could probably tell you how to make it, but I've never had so much as a sip." She was looking at the selection of titles, running her fingers over the spines of the handsomely bound volumes. If she didn't stop walking around so that damned dress swayed and touched her in places he wanted to, he was going pitch the bottle and both glasses out the window. Then he was going to grab her, toss her down to the carpet and make love to her until she was senseless. Until they were both senseless.

Beau glanced down and realized he had a death grip on the neck of the wine bottle. He set it down. "I can get you a soft drink if you'd—"

"No." She walked straight to him and took the glass. "This is fine." She took a small sip and blinked several times when the taste hit her senses. The flavor was...she couldn't find enough words to describe the taste, but her reaction was easy to interpret. It made her feel powerful and as light as air at the same time. She smiled. "I like it."

"Good. Just remember to go slow since it's your first wine experience."

Listen to him. He sounded like some overprotective father instead of a man who wanted to take her to bed. But since he preferred women with sophisticated tastes he'd simply never encountered this situation before and he didn't mind admitting a touch of discomfort. Of course, it wasn't like he was contributing to the delinquency of a minor or anything, but having wine for the first time was sort of like losing your virginity. Slow and easy always made you appreciate the experience more.

"This is a wonderful room," Lily said, taking another sip. "It would be my favorite if I lived here."

Beau smiled, pleased with her enjoyment. "For obvious reasons, of course."

"Of course. I think a room is undressed without at least one book in it, don't you?"

"Undressed. That's an interesting way to put it."

Lily smiled to herself. Once she'd seen that look of stunned appreciation on his face when she first arrived and realized he found her attractive, she'd relaxed, even began to enjoy her role as seductress. This part was fun. Of course, she wasn't naive enough to think the rest of it would be a snap, but she suspected that once she told Beau what she wanted from him, they would both be more comfortable. That thought quickly punctured a hole in her happy seductress balloon. Yes, the sooner she told him, the better. Before dinner was probably best. The right thing to do, particularly since to continue without telling was a little like she was dining under false pretenses. If her plan had any chance of success it would only be through honesty. As lovely as the evening has been so far, she couldn't afford to delude herself into thinking of it as a romantic interlude. She had to stick to her plan.

"Maybe later you'd be kind enough to show me the rest of the house. I was here once for a reception to receive a donation from your fa—Mr. Stuart, but I never saw anything but the foyer and dining room. Is the upstairs as grand as the downstairs?"

Beau almost choked on his wine. "Yeah." Just who was seducing whom here? And why was he even asking? Relax and enjoy, he told himself. "And speaking of dinner—"

"Beau, before we eat, could we talk for a moment."

"Thought that's what we'd been doing."

"Well, yes, but not...that is, there's something I'd like to discuss with you and I'd really rather do it before dinner."

He shrugged. "Go ahead."

"I...I have a confession to make. I had...have an ulterior motive for accepting your invitation."

So, she was too good to be true, he thought. When he'd walked away from her this afternoon he told himself that if she was on a mission to get information for the town she would go home disappointed. But he was the one feeling disappointed. For a while he thought she really was something special and it seemed she was just a spy. "Look, Lily—"

"No, please, let me say this before I lose my nerve. I said I had an ulterior motive and it's true. I want something from you, Beau."

"What else is new?"

"I have to be honest and tell you that, even though I've been planning this for months, I hadn't really given a lot of thought to exactly how I would do it, but—"

"So you just jumped right in like a good little citizen, huh?"

"Oh, no. I knew exactly what I was getting into."

"And you thought I would be a real pushover? Didn't they tell you what a bastard I was? No pun intended."

She didn't understand why his attitude had changed so abruptly, but she was determined to put her cards on the table. "No, I don't think you're a pushover, but I did see you as the perfect candidate and I'd hoped you would want to cooperate. I suppose I thought that because you didn't care if something sounded a little shocking—"

"Yeah, well, I've been shocking the people around here in one way or another since the day I was born. But I sure as hell didn't expect them to counter with a dirty trick."

Now she was puzzled. "Dirty trick?"

"They probably thought they had a real Trojan horse in you."

"They? They, who?"

"Whoever sent you."

"No one sent me. I just told you I'd been working toward this for months and when you arrived out of the blue...well, you just seemed like the answer to all my prayers. Not prayers, more like fate."

"How could you have worked on this for months? My father's heart attack was totally unexpected.

How could you know I would even come back to this town?"

"Oh, I didn't. But when you showed up and you fit every one of my criteria, I couldn't ignore—"

"Criteria? What criteria?"

"Experienced, available and temporary."

"Available for what?"

"Sex, of course."

Beau's mouth dropped open and he stared at her as if she'd just landed from Mars. "E...excuse me?"

"Sex." When he continued to stare, she added, "Surely, I don't have to explain sex to a man of your—"

He waved her off. "I understand about the sex part. What I don't understand is..." Beau sighed. "At the moment, not much of anything. Let me get this straight. You didn't come here to talk to me on behalf of the town's people? To find out what I intend to do with the factory?"

"Good heavens, no. I came here tonight because I decided that the only way I'm ever going to have the kind of sexual experience I want is with a man of the world."

"You decided," he said, still dumbfounded.

"Yes."

"Just like that?"

"Just like that."

"But you don't know me."

She smiled as if everything made perfect sense. "That's what makes you the ideal man."

3

HE WAS EITHER THE LUCKIEST man alive or this dream had turned into one helluva a bizarre nightmare. "You came here to ask me, a total stranger, to have sex with you?"

"Absolutely. That's the only way my plan works."

"You have a plan."

"Well, yes. I know it may sound a little strange, but—"

"Oh, no. I get one or two similar propositions every month."

"Now you're making fun of me. I assure you, Beau, this was not a frivolous decision."

"Sorry. I'm sure it wasn't. What I don't understand is, why me? Why not find some nice local guy, get married and do it the old-fashioned way?"

"Maybe you didn't hear me say, 'the kind of sexual experience I want,' or that one of the things that made you such an excellent choice was that you were temporary. I don't want an affair and I don't want to get married. I just want to have great sex without all the usual stuff."

"And the usual stuff would be...?"

"Romance, promises of undying love. This isn't about love and I don't want any kind of emotional connection. I want to have a good time for as long as it lasts without any strings, any regrets. You should know that I'm healthy and not presently in a sexual relationship. Nor have I been for at least several months."

Beau stared at her for another minute, then walked to the bar. "I need something stronger than wine," he muttered, reaching for a decanter of scotch.

"Did you say something?"

He raised the glass to his lips, took a long drink and looked her in the eyes. "You expecting me to produce a notarized statement from the board of health?"

"No. I guess not. Besides, I've taken care of protection."

"Efficient."

"This isn't something we can leave to chance."

"Damn right, it's not. The last thing I want is a little surprise wrapped in pink or blue."

"There's one more thing. I...have to ask you to promise me you'll never mention this to anyone."

"I thought you said no promises."

"This is an exception to the rules. And it's very important. In fact, my plan doesn't work without it."

He drained the last of the scotch then gazed into the bottom of the glass for a moment. "Now I see why you think I'm so 'ideal.' You need somebody who won't talk. An outsider, maybe even an outlaw, right?"

"Yes. I hope that doesn't offend you."

"Why should it? Guilty on both counts. I am most definitely an outsider and I haven't exactly lived the life of a choir boy." He poured himself another drink. "And since I'm an expert on being exiled by the righteous of Rosemont, I sure as hell understand why you don't want to be labeled an outsider."

"You'd be surprised. In some ways I'm as much an outsider as you. They just tone it down because of my family. If it was just me, I wouldn't care." She shrugged. "If it was just me, this conversation would be academic because I'd have left town long ago."

"Why don't you?"

"My mother. She suffered through a nasty scandal years ago and I don't think her health could handle another. That's why your promise is so important."

"Has it crossed your mind that you've put yourself in a sort of moral cross fire? The reason I fit your plan is that you think I'm a real son of a bitch. But if I'm a son of a bitch then what makes you think I'll keep my promise?"

"Oh," Lily said, unable to deny the logic of his statement. "I hadn't thought about it from that point of view."

"Don't get me wrong, darlin'. I've always been a big fan of having your cake and eating it, too. But if you can't be sure, then maybe now is the time to cut your losses." Again, he was playing hero. Why didn't he just keep his mouth shut and let them both get what they wanted.

She stared at him and he could almost see her going through her options, balancing the pros and cons. Finally, she said, "No. I don't want to cut my losses, as you put it."

"You sure?"

"Do I have your promise?"

"Before I give you my answer, I'd like to know what you meant by 'the kind of sexual encounter you want'? Exactly what kind is that? Are we talking kinky, here? I mean, if you're into leather and handcuffs then I'm not—"

"Oh, no! Nothing like that. I just want..."

"What?"

"Excitement. My, uh, experience is limited. I want to—" she almost said "make love" but stopped herself "—have sex with a man who knows how. Really knows. A man who is more interested in pleasure than just pleasuring himself."

Beau nodded. Sounded good to him and Lord knew she looked good enough to make a normal man doubt his sanity. She must have had a less than satisfactory lover, or possibly lovers. Probably some impatient, fumbling buck who didn't recognize a diamond in the rough when it was right under his nose. Poor baby. He guessed she'd had just enough exposure to know something was missing and enough guts to go looking for it. Even so, he wondered if she had any real clue about what she was asking.

"What makes you think I really know?"

"I can't believe you're asking me that. With your confidence, slash, arrogance? You don't strike me as the kind of man who continually needs his ego flattered."

"I'm also a big fan of ego flattering, particularly when it's mine, but how do you know it's not all blow and no go?"

"By your reputation. It's well-known that you've dated tons of women. Every time I see your picture in the Richmond paper you've got a different woman on your arm. You frequently make the local gossip column."

"That doesn't mean I'm Casanova reincarnated. For all you know those women could just be interested in me for my money."

"Are you trying to tell me that you're not a ladies' man after all?"

Beau smiled. "Well, with the exception of you, they're not exactly beating down my door, but I do all right."

"Then, you'll do it? And promise to keep my secret?"

"What happens to your plan if I back out?"

She'd never considered that he might say no and

the prospect was more disappointing than she could have imagined. Funny, she thought, how quickly perspectives change. Yesterday her knowledge of Beau consisted of one glimpse and a lot of gossip. More fiction than fact. Today, even though she'd only been with him for less than an hour, she couldn't imagine being intimate with any man but him. Lily took a deep breath, releasing it slowly. "I'll have to find another man." She didn't want to, but there was no other choice. "It may take a while, but I'm sure I'll find someone. Eventually."

His smile kicked into a wicked grin. "Careful, you'll dent my ego."

"I'm sorry. I really hoped it would be you, but—"

"But if not, you're determined to make this happen."

"Absolutely."

He seemed to consider her for a moment and then abruptly nodded. "All right. I guess once in a blue moon you gotta do something wild," he said. "You have my promise."

"Thank you." As he walked toward her, still wearing that wicked grin, she wondered if she hadn't just made a bargain with the devil.

He stopped right in front of her, then slipped his hand to the back of her neck. Slowly he pulled her to him until her knees bumped his. The contact was electric. "Feel like you just cut a deal with the devil?"

"As a matter of fact—"

"You did," he assured her a second before his mouth took hers.

She'd been kissed before, on more than a couple of occasions and by adult men other than relatives. She'd probably read hundreds of descriptions of kisses, seen several hundred screen kisses.

But none of it could have prepared her for this kiss. Beau's kiss. Or her response.

His mouth touched hers, and if he hadn't been holding her, she would have jumped at the shock—a sudden, hot burst of electricity like the high voltage shot delivered when you touch a doorknob after walking across a thick carpet. Just as suddenly the shock disappeared and the world, her world, tilted on its axis, sending her spinning off into another universe. A universe of need and hunger. Hers. For him. Desire hit her suddenly and hard. Primitive and powerful it ripped through her, stripping away everything but the moment, the need. It was so sudden, so overwhelming she felt as though there had been an explosion and she was standing at ground zero. Starting at her feet, the blast ignited, roaring upward like rockets preparing for lift-off. Raw, urgent desire shot and sizzled through her bloodstream setting off microexplosions along every nerve ending. Her body literally vibrated with sexual energy. And just like tasting the wine, she might have to search for the right words, but her reaction was easy to describe.

She liked it. Loved it. Couldn't wait for more. *Oh, please let there be more,* she thought.

Beau had intended the kiss to tease and entice, but something unexpected happened the moment their lips met. If he didn't know better he would swear he'd just touched a live wire while standing in water. Whether it was the shock of her immediate and powerful response, or his own, the highly charged combination seemed to fry his brain. All he could think about was to keep on kissing her. Maybe forever. The feel, taste and scent of her filled his mind and body to the exclusion of all else.

She was silk in his arms, but raw silk. She tasted like honey, only wild honey. And her fragrance went straight to his head in a way the scotch would never be able to. Whoever the man was that had disappointed her, he must have been deaf, dumb and blind. Beau had no such handicap. This was no delicate hothouse flower. This was a woman in full bloom and he intended to enjoy the blossom while he could.

Without breaking the kiss he all but carried her to the sofa near the fireplace. Using one knee to brace them, he leaned her back and down until they were half reclined, half sprawled on the sofa. Beau pulled her on top of him and kept right on kissing her. Not that he had a choice. He'd been starving before but he'd never craved food the way he craved her lips. While what remained of rational thought insisted he go easy, desire said to hell with easy. If just kissing her was driving him this mad he shuddered, and thrilled, to think what making love to her would do.

"B-Beau," she gasped when they finally broke the kiss. "I—I—"

"You talk too much." And he kissed her again. First teasing, then demanding, he nibbled and plucked at her mouth. Then he took the kiss deeper still, his hands eagerly exploring the softness of her shoulders, the enticing nip at her waist, the firmness of her hips. He couldn't get enough of her.

While Lily clung to the last fragments of reason she reveled in the whirlwind of sensation that heightened with every touch of his hand, every stroke of his tongue. She had no idea it could be so intense, so wild and all consuming, yet so free and liberating. The more she took, the more she wanted and the more he gave. Even though she'd never made love, instinctively she knew she'd taken steps down a road with no turning back. And she was happy, eager—and scared. But that last pesky bit of reason revolving around two foil-wrapped packets in her purse refused to be ignored.

"I need..."

"Yes."

"We have to—"

"We will, we will," he said between ravenous kisses. In the past he'd prided himself on taking his time with women, enjoying them to the fullest. Now he couldn't touch her, kiss her fast enough. Need was like a knife in his gut. He'd never felt this kind of mind-robbing desire for any woman. He had to be inside her as much as he had to breathe to survive.

"Are you protected?"

"Protection...yes—"

"That's all I want to know."

She was trying to form the word *stop* in her brain when he abruptly shifted positions. In one incredibly swift move he sat up, pulling her across his lap then lifted her, resettling her astride him. Lily gasped. Half a heartbeat later she was bare to the waist. Then he leaned forward and took a nipple into his mouth and sucked.

She almost cried out with the intense explosion of sensation. Her last rational thought was that she was going to die of pleasure. After that there was nothing but feeling. No thought, no reason. Nothing except his lips on her breasts. She gave herself over to his hot mouth and her hotter flesh craving more. She didn't care about yesterday or tomorrow. Only the pull of his mouth, the magic of his tongue. And whatever ecstasy lay in store. Whatever that was, she didn't know or care, so long as it was more. So long as he didn't stop.

"Sweet," he rasped, his greedy mouth moving from one nipple to the other. "Taste so sweet. I want you...so bad I can't breathe."

"Yes...yes..."

"I have to see you. All of you."

He slid from the sofa to the floor taking her with him and before her bottom touched the carpet he had whisked the slip-dress over her head and discarded it. Wearing nothing but her naughty new panties and the scent of desire, she faced him, so caught up in her own hunger the thought of being shy or coy never entered her head. All she saw was her own need reflected in his eyes.

She was a fire burning only for him and he wanted nothing more than to plunge into the flame and let it consume them both. He caged her face in his hands and proceeded to devour her mouth until her lips were swollen and pouty. It wasn't enough. Not nearly enough. Gazing into her eyes he ran his hands over her shoulders, down her arms to her narrow waist, pulling her to him for another mind-robbing kiss.

His mouth was a hot, greedy scavenger. It was wonderful. It was wicked. But it wasn't fair. She wanted to touch him, taste him. She wanted to sink into him until they melted together. She wanted the rest of the unknown pleasure that he could give her.

"Now you," she barely managed to whisper as she reached for the buttons on his shirt. "I want to see you, touch you."

Beau was way ahead of her and by the time she finished with buttons he had removed his belt and unzipped his pants. He shrugged out of his shirt, stopping only for occasional quick kisses accompanied by the sweet sound of a moan.

"Hurry," she whispered.

He wanted to hear her ask for more. Demand more. And he wanted to meet her demands over and over until their was nothing left but sweat and satisfaction. To that end he stood up, shoved underwear and slacks down at the same time and kicked them off. Then he pulled her up to him.

She looked down then back into his eyes, her own now heavy-lidded with desire. She wanted to remember every second, to etch every taste, touch and sound of this moment forever in her brain. "Now?"

"Soon, darlin'. Soon."

With both hands he cupped her breasts, coaxing her body slightly forward until her nipples touched his chest and his sex met hers. Only the thin barrier of lace prevented flesh from touching flesh. As if to make up for such a cruel hesitation he moved her torso from side to side, stroking his chest against her hard nipples. Back and forth.

"Please," she begged. "Oh, please..."

In answer to her plea he slipped one hand around to the small of her back, holding her while the other hand slipped inside her panties to cup her.

This time she did cry out. Or maybe it was a moan. She didn't know, didn't care. Her skin was damp and fevered. A dark, primitive need speared through her, carrying her up to some high place of pleasure where she teetered on the edge.

"Is this what you want?"

He stroked her and with every touch lightning streaked through her.

"Y-yes."

"But more. You want more, don't you? Lots more."

"More...yes. All of it."

"Easy, darlin'."

But she didn't want to take it easy. She wanted more of his kisses, more of his sizzling touches, everything he had to give. And then she wanted to give him all of her, everything she was.

"You want to feel me?"

"Yes, yes."

He hooked his thumbs in the waistband of her panties and pushed them down, working them off first one leg then the other. "Now? You want to feel me now?"

"Oh...oh, yes."

He put his hands under her arms and lifted her up just enough to slip his hard, hot sex between her legs without yet entering her. And then he started to move.

The unexpected shock of her first climax ripped through her body and mind, leaving her weak and powerful, sated and starved all at the same time. And she wanted it to go on forever.

Beau wanted to give her the full measure of pleasure she'd asked for but he wasn't sure how much longer he could hold out. But the way she was moving against him on her own now he didn't think he would have to wait long. In direct opposition to the almost overwhelming urge to toss her onto her back and plunge inside her, he laid her gently onto the floor.

"Beautiful," he whispered, running his hands over her breasts and belly. Again, he cupped her, only this time he didn't stop with just touching. Now he stroked and petted, all the while suckling her breasts. She squirmed, arching her back, eager for another delicious explosion. And when he slipped a finger inside her, swollen and dewy with need, he felt her body stiffen for a moment. Then she went wild. Writhing beneath him, hips pumping, she strained for more. Mindless with his own need for release the last of his control snapped.

"I've got to be inside you."

He pushed her legs apart, and plunged deep. Then froze.

"Lily?"

The split second of pressure she'd felt disappeared beneath a wave of pleasure so intense it threatened to overwhelm her. But he stopped and she couldn't allow that. She had to have more, more, more. "Please," she whimpered, nearly insane with needing him.

"Lily, wait—"

"No." Giving over to pure animal instinct she gripped his hips, arching upward. Once, twice and then she lost count. All that mattered was the feel of him inside her.

Whatever caution he intended was lost. He was helpless against her frantic demand for satisfaction and he drove deep inside her, meeting her thrust for thrust, their sweat-slick bodies keeping time to the ages-old rhythm of mating. And then an explosion like a supernova burst inside them then rippled out in pure, shuddering satisfaction.

THEY FELL ASLEEP on the floor.

Beau woke up first to find her snuggled trustingly against him, her head on his chest and one leg entwined with his, sleeping like an innocent child. But she was certainly no child, and now, thanks to him, she was no longer innocent. Guilt slashed at his conscience. He should never have agreed to her request. Regardless of how matter-of-fact she'd been about what she wanted,

Gazing down at her, Beau couldn't decide if his anger was stronger than his desire to have her again. Part of him wanted to shake her until her teeth rattled for not stopping him, not telling him she was a virgin. Another part of him wanted to shake her awake and do everything he'd just done, plus more, and for the rest of the night. Almost as a preventive measure he reached up, pulled an afghan from the sofa and gently settled it over them. She sighed and snuggled closer.

He still couldn't believe she hadn't told him. Then again, if she had he couldn't honestly say he could have stopped. Not with her bucking beneath him like a wild thing and begging for satisfaction. And she had been satisfied. He'd seen to that. In fact, he couldn't remember when he'd enjoyed a woman more, or felt better afterward himself. God, but she was sweet. Who would have thought that someone as jaded as he could find so much pleasure in a virgin? Certainly not him. He wondered if she would be shocked to learn she wasn't the only one with a "first" tonight. She was his first virgin. And the way his heart had damn near stopped when he'd pushed inside her, she'd be his last. Despite his shock, despite a flash of fear, her determination had never wavered. She wanted him, wanted their bargain.

But that still didn't give her the right to deliberately withhold... Beau stifled such self-righteous macho thinking. No one had twisted his arm. She'd told him her experience was limited and he'd never questioned how limited. He'd never questioned it because he hadn't wanted to know. He'd never once asked if she was a beginner, intermediate or advanced student of the art of love.

Love?

What did love have to do with this? It had no place

in what had happened. She'd said that straight out. This wasn't about love and she wasn't interested in any kind of emotional connection. Didn't want it. As far as he was concerned, ditto. Big-time. So, how had the word love crept into his brain? Beau shook his head as if to shake it free of the thoughts. Didn't matter. They were consenting adults enjoying each other. Period. But it did matter. Call it pride or machismo but there was something wrong with her casual attitude. Dammit, she was too much woman to have to ask a man for sex. The thought that he might not have been the man to receive the gift she'd offered so freely bothered him. More than it should have. More than he wanted it to. That fact alone scared and angered him.

She stirred in his arms, slowly coming awake. "Beau?"

"I'm here."

Lily leaned her head back and looked up into his dark blue eyes. "Are you angry?"

"Damn straight," he said, calmly. Maybe a little too calmly. He tossed the afghan aside, grabbed his shorts and stepped into them. He started for the bar, but stopped, turned to face her. "Why didn't you tell me you'd never been with a man?"

"Because you would have stopped and that's not what I wanted," she said, reaffirming his thoughts. "I told you that I hadn't made this decision lightly. I didn't lie to you and I wouldn't have even if you had asked me point-blank. This would have happened sooner or later, so you have nothing to feel guilty about. I asked for this."

"Guilty?" he asked, slightly irritated that she had pegged his feelings so quickly and accurately. "Why should I feel guilty, I only—"

"You shouldn't."

"I mean it's not like I lured you to my house with plans to seduce you or anything."

"Quite the opposite. I seduced you."

"Well, I wasn't exactly resisting. No man in his right mind can resist a woman with real desire. Certainly not the kind you displayed."

"Then I was okay?"

"You have to ask? Well, yes, considering you have nothing to compare it to—" he shrugged "—I suppose you do. Where the hell did you learn to respond to a man like that?"

"Books."

Beau's eyes widened. "Books?"

"I read a lot. Always have. And I retain a lot."

"Darlin' there's not a book written that could describe what just happened. I'd say you've got a natural aptitude."

"That's good, isn't it?"

He grinned. "From my point of view it's fantastic."

"And mine."

Lily watched him, awed by so much masculine beauty. She doubted he would appreciate knowing she thought him beautiful, but he was. A magnificent male animal and she blessed fate for her good fortune. Now, it was up to her to make the best of that good fortune. Not a hardship, she thought. Not at all. Just seeing him standing there, hard muscles and power, her body flushed hot from head to toe. Her breasts tingled with the memory of his mouth, his tongue working their magic.

"I wanted you," she said simply.

"Like hell on fire."

"I still do."

Beau stared at her. "You're unbelievable. I've never been with a woman like you. Are you always so honest, so up-front?"

A compliment. Halfhearted, perhaps, but she was sure it was a compliment. "Yes. Does that mean you're not angry anymore?"

"I should be."

"But you're not." When he shook his head she smiled. "Good, because I think... I mean if you want to, we could do it again."

"I'm not sure we should—"

She stood up, leaving the afghan behind.

"Uh..." He tried to remember the rest of his protest, but seeing her walking naked toward him blew it right out of his head. That walk, that sexy little sway, was arresting when she was fully clothed. In the nude she was too much for a mere mortal man.

She stopped. "You don't want to?"

"No. I mean, yes, I do, but..."

"But what?"

"Are you sure you wouldn't rather wait. You know, sort of rest."

"Why?"

"Give me a break here. I'm trying to be the gentleman I should've been two hours ago. I was concerned that you might be...a little tender. After all, it was your first time and there is such a thing as too much, too fast."

Lily sighed with relief. For a moment she thought their affair was all over practically before it began. "Don't you think that should be my call?"

"Yeah, but..."

She walked right up to him and put her arms around his neck, pressing her body to his. "Then you'll just have to take my word for it. I feel wonderful."

Beau ran his hands over her back and down to cup her saucy backside. He urged her closer. "You feel incredible."

She kissed his chest. "So do you."

"How soon do you have to leave?"

"Hmm. A few minutes."

He leaned her back far enough to trail kisses down her throat to her breasts. "Good thing I work well under pressure." His mouth closed around a pebbled nipple and sucked hard. Instantly her body went taut, then as pliable as warm wax.

"Oh, oh," she moaned. Unable to stand not having him closer, she slid her hands to his buttocks and pulled him against her. She ground her hips against his erection. "Maybe there's no rush."

"The hell there isn't."

He had every intention of taking her upstairs, but this time they were lucky to make it to the sofa before the frenzied rush of white-hot, mind-robbing desire overcame them.

Lily thought she knew what to expect but it wasn't like the first time. It was wilder, hotter, more intense and more shattering when the climax came. Vaguely she wondered if every time would be a little different and hoped she had enough strength to find out.

Afterward as Beau walked her to the door, Lily felt awkward for the first time since she'd stepped inside the Stuart mansion. How did she end the evening? Shake his hand. A good-night kiss and... No. No kisses or she might never get home. It would be bliss to spend the night in Beau's arms, but he hadn't even mentioned when he wanted to see her again, much less spending the night.

"Well." She took a deep breath when they reached the door. "I guess I'd better go—"

"Are you free tomorrow?"

Her heart soared for a second before she realized the following day was Sunday. "No. We, my mother and I, always have dinner with my aunt Pauline on Sundays. And, of course, I have to be in the library by eight Monday morning." Lily frowned. "I told you that I hadn't thought this whole thing out in detail."

"And?"

"And I suddenly realized that inventing excuses to go to Richmond can only last so long before my mother begins to question them."

"So how do you plan to handle the situation?"

"I'm not sure, but I'll work it out." She looked into his eyes. "I will work it out."

Beau grinned. "I do appreciate a woman with determination."

"Of course, I don't expect you to rearrange your schedule to suit me. You probably have a lot to do concerning your fa—" She caught herself. "Well, the estate and everything."

"It's okay, Lily. He *was* my biological father."

"Despite all the rumors, I have no idea how you felt about your father. Neither does anyone else in this town for that matter. Not really."

"Let's just say he wasn't on my Christmas list and leave it at that. But you're right. I have a lot to do concerning his estate, beginning with this—" he gestured toward the foyer and grand staircase "—big old barn of a house."

"Are you going to sell it?"

"Not sure I can. The damn thing is so old, and needs so much work I may have to bulldoze it."

"Oh, no, Beau. You can't do that. Why this house

was built before the Civil War. It has a wonderful history."

"Most of it fiction."

"Absolutely not."

"What makes you think so?"

"Because I'm vice president of the local historical society. Believe me, this house has a rich heritage and should to be preserved."

"You don't say." He glanced around the foyer, dining room and staircase. When he looked back at her there was a definite gleam in his eyes. "That's very interesting."

"I'm glad you think so... Why are you looking at me like that?"

"Because, darlin'—" he pulled her into his arms "—I just may have the answer to your problem." He kissed her deeply.

They'd had sex twice. Hot, demanding, no-holds-barred sex, yet she responded to him as if they were longtime lovers. She couldn't resist him, could only melt in his arms. She simply had no defense against the hunger he ignited. A hunger that was uncontrollable once unleashed. It took all her willpower to end the kiss.

"My problem?" she said, fighting the urge to step back into his arms.

Beau started to reach for her, but stopped. She had to be exhausted, yet he knew if he kissed her again where it would lead. He'd promised to keep their time together a secret and keeping her out all night to satisfy his own uncontrollable lust wouldn't get their bargain off to a good start.

"I'll tell you tomorrow."

"But you can't call me. How will you—"

"Let me worry about how. Go home and sleep well."

Sleep well, she thought, driving home a few moments later. How could she sleep well or otherwise when all she wanted was to turn her car around and go straight back into his arms? Her life had changed tonight. Who cared about something as inconsequential as a few hours sleep?

Lily smiled. As bargains with the devil went, this one was off to a roaring start.

4

LILY WOKE UP SUNDAY MORNING still feeling as if she was in the middle of a dream. A wonderful dream, she thought, stretching lazily. A dream she hoped lasted right up until the very moment Beau had to leave Rosemont. After last night she didn't want to think about him leaving, even though she knew it was inevitable. This wasn't a romance, she reminded herself. It was just sex. And what sex. Once hadn't been enough, and...

She sat straight up in bed. Twice. They'd done it twice.

Without the condoms.

Her heart shot into her throat and for a moment she thought she might be sick to her stomach. How could she have been so careless? How could she have allowed herself to lose control to the point where she forgot all about the doctor's warning?

Are you protected?

And she had been so deep into her own need she couldn't even tell him to stop long enough to use a condom. What an idiot she'd been. A greedy, inexperienced idiot. And if that wasn't bad enough, she'd been careless not once, but twice. Monumental stupidity. The urge to scream out her frustration was cut short by a knock at her door.

"Lily, dear," came her mother's voice through the door. "I didn't hear you dressing for church. Everything all right?"

"Uh, yes. But...uh, I've got a wretched headache. You and Aunt Pauline will have to go without me today." There was a long silence before her mother answered.

"Maybe I should stay home and make sure—"

"No, Mom. Please go on without me, I'll be fine."

"Well, if you're sure."

"Yes, I'm sure."

"All right, then. I'll check on you when I get home."

"Fine. Thanks, Mom."

A few minutes later she heard her mother leave for church and breathed a sigh of relief. But there was no relief from the glaring stupidity of what she'd done.

What if she'd gotten pregnant? Could a woman get pregnant the first time? Surely not.

"Oh, don't be silly. Of course you can."

But she wasn't. She couldn't be. That would ruin everything.

Lily doubled her hands into fists, hit the rumpled bedcovers and started crying. Not only had she put herself in a precarious position, but what about Beau? He'd agreed to a brief encounter, not fathering a child. And what about her mother? A pregnant, unmarried daughter. The scandal would probably kill her. The enormity of her mistake washed over Lily like an icy tidal wave. "Oh, please," she whispered a prayer. "I made a mistake but don't make others suffer for it."

She cried until there was nothing left to cry. Raised to believe self-pity was an unacceptable excuse for not facing responsibility, she finally pulled herself together and dried her eyes. Falling to pieces wouldn't help. If last night resulted in—she took an unsteady breath—her becoming pregnant then the damage was done and there was no use crying over spilt milk. If not, then she had to make double sure that Beau used protection from now on. But then how did she explain not using a condom last night? A part of her wanted to tell him the truth, felt he deserved the truth. But if her prayer was answered and nothing came of her mistake, why make him miserable unnecessarily? She just had to make sure...

No, double sure. That's how she would handle the issue of not having him use a condom last night. She would tell him that she was on the Pill, but hadn't been taking them very long. So, to be double sure nothing happened she would ask him to use a condom. And it wouldn't even be a lie.

And what about that spilt milk? her conscience wanted to know. She would face that reality when, and if, it became one. And she would do it on her own. That much she did know.

"AH, MISS MATTHEWS."

Lily glanced from her computer screen behind the library's main check-in desk and smiled. "Good morning, Mayor Caldwell. It's nice to see—" Her jaw dropped when Beau walked through the door to stand beside the mayor.

"Uh, Lily, I don't think you've met Beau Stuart. Beau, this is Miss Lily Matthews, our head librarian and vice president of our local historical society."

Beau shook her hand. "Miss Matthews, delighted."

Stunned to see Beau and befuddled to see him with the mayor, she wasn't so shocked that she didn't feel her body respond.

"I wonder if could we talk in your office?" Caldwell asked.

"Of course."

As soon as they were inside her office, Caldwell closed the door. Lily's gaze shot to Beau but his eyes gave her no clue as to was happening.

"Mr. Stuart—" the mayor began.

"Beau, please."

Caldwell smiled. "Yes. Mr.—Beau, has come to me with a very generous offer. He wants to donate the Stuart mansion to the city of Rosemont to be preserved as a museum. And since the house was originally built by your family, and considering your position in the historical society, he hopes that you will consent to oversee the project."

"Project?"

"That's the most exciting part. Beau is willing to donate up to one million dollars to restore the house to its original condition. Isn't that remarkable, Lily?"

"Very generous indeed, Mr.—"

"Mind if we leave off the formalities? I'm a pretty down-to-earth guy once you get to know me."

"Well, now that we're all comfortable, Beau, why don't you tell Lily **your** idea?"

"Oh, I don't want to steal your thunder, Ben."

"Nonsense. This was your idea and I think you should get the credit."

Lily had never seen the mayor so flustered, but then a million dollars can fluster anyone.

"To make it short and sweet, Lily, I would like for you to take complete charge of restoring your family's home. Now, I'm aware that you have a full-time job—"

"Oh, don't worry about that. Lily has an excellent assistant librarian who can take up the slack here."

Beau grinned. "Thanks, Ben." Then he turned his full attention to Lily. "It's a big job, and I'll just tell you up-front that I'd require a lot of your time over the next couple of weeks, including some evenings. Will that be a problem?"

"Oh, absolutely—"

"I can answer for myself," she told Caldwell. Lily almost laughed out loud at the panicked expression on the mayor's face. He was probably terrified that she would refuse, based on Beau's reputation alone. "That's not a problem at all, Beau. I'd be happy to help with the project, and speaking for the city, thank you."

Beau shrugged. "Believe me, Lily, I was happy to do it. And I'm sure I'll be very pleased with your efforts."

"I'll do my best to make certain everything is worked out to your satisfaction."

"I'll leave it all in your expert hands. If you're satisfied, that's good enough for me."

"Well—" Ben Caldwell rubbed his hands together "—since this is settled, why don't we go over to the bank and—"

"Don't worry about it, Ben," Beau said. "I'll have my attorney get in touch with your office this afternoon. He'll handle all the boring details at no expense to the city. All I ask is that we keep this under wraps for now. I'm not sure how the town will react to my gesture so I'd rather keep it low-key for a while."

"On behalf of the city of Rosemont," Ben said. "I'd like to say how grateful we are and how much we appreciate your generosity."

"I don't know about the whole town being grateful. Most of them hate my guts. But, then, I didn't do it for gratitude. The house should be preserved as a part of our history. Don't you agree, Lily?"

"Unquestionably."

"Thank you, Lily. And now we won't keep you any longer," said the mayor and went to usher Beau out.

"If it's all the same to you, Ben, I'd like to hear some of Lily's ideas." He smiled at her. "If you have the time."

"For something this important, I'll make time."

Moments later Beau had seen the mayor out the office door and closed it behind him. When he turned to face Lily he was grinning. "How'd I do, darlin'?"

"Do you have any business concerns in Alaska," she asked.

"Not that I know of. Why?"

"Because you could sell ice cubes to the Inuit."

The grin widened. "Right now I'm more interested in heat than cold. Your heat." He crooked a finger. "C'mere."

"What for?" she asked, already walking toward him. She stopped right in front of him.

"So I can do this." He yanked her into his arms and his mouth came down hard on hers.

One touch. That's all it took for her to go weak in the knees and melt all over him like hot fudge over vanilla ice cream.

"Is there a lock on this door?"

"Behave yourself," she said between kisses, only half hoping he would.

"Not my style, darlin'. Besides, that's not what you really want from me, is it?"

"No," she said.

"And you know why?" He nipped her bottom lip then ran his tongue over it.

She sighed with pleasure. "Why?"

Beau caged her face in his hands, drawing back enough to look into her eyes. "Because deep down you know this is real and honest. It's not misbehaving, it's living, wanting life to be as full and rich as it can be. Should be."

"Yes."

This time when he kissed her he lingered, tasted, coaxed. He kissed her gently, sweetly, but with every bit of passion and need that he had before. When he finally broke the kiss she almost cried out at the loss of sweetness.

"And now, Miss Vice President, are you ready to do some research?"

"Absolutely. And if I may so, the story of donating the house was brilliant."

Beau drew back. "You really must think I'm a son of a bitch. It wasn't a story. I am donating the house and I do want you to help."

"But I thought—"

"That I was just doing it so you would have a legitimate reason for coming to my house."

"Well...yes."

"It's a double-barrel deal. You get a good excuse and I get a tax write-off." He drew her back into his arms. "Now about that research. Can you start tonight?"

"You're serious."

"Of course I am. What time—"

"Beau, you gave away a million dollars without blinking an eye?"

"Told you. Tax write-off."

"But the house. Your father's house."

"Lily, that house means nothing to me. In fact, it represents a part of my life I'd just as soon forget. But I hate waste, so turning the house over to the town and keeping a part of history is a good thing."

"It's certainly a good thing for Rosemont, and I'm sure the city council will want to show their appreciation—"

"No," Beau said.

"But—"

"No. And I'm depending on you to make them understand. I don't want appreciation or recognition." He kissed her again. "Now, why are we talking about a house when there are much more important topics? Like how soon we can do a repeat of last night."

"Well, since you've made that possible now, I guess we could see each other tonight. But, Beau, just as you're serious about donating the house, I'm serious about doing my part."

"So, you're coming over to dig through old pictures and the family bible—" he ran a hand over her hip and pressed her to him "—rather than slip into my bed?"

The mental image of the two of them naked in his bed made her shiver. Desire flooded her body. "I just—" He moved her hips from side to side, still pressing. "Uh, I, uh, just think I should do some work. First."

He grinned. "Seven o'clock. No, make it six-thirty. We'll take a peek in the attic, have dinner, then we'll have each other. How does that sound?"

"G-good." It sounded better than good. It sounded deliciously full of erotic promise.

"Damn straight it does." He gave her one last bone-melting kiss, then started to leave. "We're going into the attic, so wear jeans." When he got to the door he turned back to her. "The tightest pair you own. I wanna see you wiggle out of them." Then he was gone.

Along with him most of her ability to reason had left, too, she feared. All it took was one touch, one kiss and she was mindless, nothing but feelings, need. Lily walked to her desk and flopped down in her chair. She should concentrate on the mountain of work on her desk, the orders for new books and a hundred other tasks, but all she could think about was tonight. All she could think about was Beau's kisses, his body and more hot, wild sex.

"HEY THERE, DARLIN'," Beau said when he opened his front door at a quarter to seven.

"Sorry, I'm late." He was wearing jeans and a T-shirt that defined his muscular arms and chest, He was so gorgeous he made her mouth water. "The explanation to my mother and aunt turned out to be longer than I expected and…difficult." It was a gross understatement.

"Trouble?" he asked as she stepped into the foyer.

"They wanted me to refuse to help with the project. I spent fifteen minutes trying to convince them of how much the town stood to gain from your donation."

"But they didn't agree."

"Let's just say they're reluctant for me to get involved with you, even for something as worthwhile as this house."

"Is that going to be a problem?"

"I won't lie and say it's not, but they know I've made the decision to help and I won't go back on my word. My aunt is a natural-born busybody and worrier. Unfortunately she can also be something of a nag. My mom is the calm one, but as I told you, she's been hurt, so she tends to be overly cautious where I'm concerned, particularly when it comes to the possibility of gossip."

"Exactly what you want to avoid. And I can't blame you."

"I'm glad you understand."

"I do. Now, you ready for the attic?"

"I was sort of hoping for a hello kiss first."

Slowly he leaned down and ever so lightly brushed his lips over hers. When she reached for him he drew back.

Disappointed, Lily blinked. "Is something wrong?"

Beau grinned. "No."

"Then why did you stop?"

"Because if I kiss you again we'll never make it to the attic, much less dinner. Anticipation is part of the game."

Her eyes sparked with fire. "I've had it up to here with anticipation. Ever since I looked up and saw you in the library this morning, kissing you has been just about all I could think about. I've had a whole day of anticipation, and I'm sick to death of it."

"Easy, darlin'. We've got time." But his body was telling him otherwise.

Lily shook her head. "If you don't kiss me right this moment, I won't be responsible for my actions."

"Is that so?"

"There's no telling what might happen."

Beau warmed to the teasing. "For instance?"

"Things like smothering you with kisses."

"A fate worst that death."

"Or, I could wrap my arms around you," she said, demonstrating her intention, "press my body to yours and—"

He pulled her to him. "Not sure I could withstand such an attack. Guess I better surrender."

"Just shut up and kiss me."

She didn't have to ask again. Like her, he'd thought of little else today but having her in his arms, in his bed. He'd lost count of the number of times he'd caught himself daydreaming about this very instant, about the moment he could touch her, taste her. Why was it, he wondered as his mouth took hers, that after only one night she was under his skin. He couldn't get enough of her, didn't want to. That thought alone should have set off warning bells, but he was too busy kissing her to notice.

Why was it, she thought vaguely, losing herself in his kiss, that no matter how many times they kissed she felt that same intense sensual shock that she'd felt with their first kiss? That same earth-shattering electricity that went through her body like lightning, leaving a fire he ignited and only he could control. She reached for the buttons on his shirt, ready for more flames.

He captured her hands, held them while he feasted on her mouth, then kissed his way to her earlobe. Lily moaned. "You're making me crazy."

"We're even. You're making me hard."

She sighed and melted against him. "Good... good."

"Yeah." He returned to devour her mouth. Finally he regained enough control to end the kiss.

"Don't stop."

"If I don't, I'm going to take you right here on this cold marble floor."

"I'm game."

Beau tried to laugh, but it came out husky and a little raw. "Don't tell me. You read it in a book."

"Several."

Her guileless honesty made her response that much more erotic. Despite that, he shook his head. "Oh, no. I promised myself we would make it to a bed and I intend to keep—"

She pulled one hand free and slid it down to his waist then around to his rear. "Sure?"

"You weren't kidding about that attack, were you?"

She almost said, all's fair in love and war, but stopped herself. "Are you surrendering?"

It took more than a little willpower, but he stepped away. "Let's call it a strategic retreat."

"He who runs away," she quoted, "lives to fight another day."

"You got it." He leaned down and gave her a quick kiss. "Just marking my place for later." Then he took her arm and led her upstairs.

As they stepped inside the attic a few moments

later, Beau flicked on a light. "Behold," he said, "the dusty remnants of your heritage and mine."

Despite the cool spring evening outside, the attic was hot, the air stuffy, but it didn't dampen Lily's excitement. "This is great!" she said, her eager gaze scanning the stacks of boxes, trunks, old furniture and paintings. A real treasure trove of the past. Rowland Stuart had only owned the house for the last thirty-five years, and she could tell some of the items were modern. But judging by the amount of dust and aging, most of it probably belonged to her family.

"There's no telling what we'll find in all of this. Could be journals, letters, birth and death records." She turned to Beau. "I'm so excited. I can't thank you enough."

"I'm jealous."

"What?" The warmth of the attic forced her to remove her jacket. "Why?"

"Thought I was the only one to put a sparkle in your eyes. Now I've got a rival."

"Don't tease. It's just that I'm surprised your father didn't get rid of most of this stuff."

"He was usually too busy making money to think about anything else. Or anybody."

"I suppose. And his wife spent a lot of her time in Baltimore, from what I've read. Then she died young."

"I was almost five, I think. I remember he called

my mother to the house and when she came home she was crying."

"You think she expected him to marry her?" When she saw the flash of pain in his eyes she wanted to cry. "I'm sorry, Beau. I shouldn't have asked such a personal question."

"No." He sighed. "You hit the nail on the head. That's exactly what she expected. Not that she would ever admit how much it hurt her. That was the day she told me we were on our own. And that was the day I started hating him. This house. This town."

"I'm so sorry that you and your mother had to suffer."

"Funny, she didn't look at it that way."

"You mean your mother?"

"She never got over him. In fact, she still talked about how much she loved him right up until the day she died." Beau shook his head. "Didn't understand it then and I still don't."

"Maybe that was enough for her."

"What do you mean? The man humiliated her."

"You say she never stopped loving him."

"Yeah."

"Maybe loving him the way she obviously did was the most important thing for her. Without it she wouldn't have had you, so maybe it was enough."

"The better-to-have-loved-and-lost theory?"

"Something like that."

"It might be okay for some, but not for me. It took

a while, but I finally put him and everything that happened behind me."

"Is that why you wanted to donate the house? So there wouldn't be any reminders of him?"

"Shouldn't I be on a couch for these questions?"

Lily knew when she was being shut out. Goodness knew her mother had done it often enough. She'd distanced herself from the past the way Beau was doing now. Don't ask, don't tell. Don't remember, don't hurt.

"I'm prying, aren't I? Again, I apologize."

He shrugged. "It's okay. Now you understand why I didn't want any surprise bundles. This world doesn't need any more illegitimate kids running around."

"Uh, speaking of that," she said, knowing she wouldn't get a better opportunity to bring up the subject of protection. "Since we both want to make sure that nothing like that happens, I was wondering if tonight when we... I mean, the next time—"

"If you're asking, will the next time be tonight, it will."

"Well, I was hoping you wouldn't mind using extra protection, just to be sure."

He lifted her hand to his lips. "My pleasure. Our pleasure."

"I brought—"

"Don't worry. I've got my own supply."

The already stuffy attic suddenly became stifling,

or was it just the touch of his mouth on her skin that sent the temperature soaring? Across her collarbone she could feel the perspiration dampen the neck of her cotton T-shirt. Beau wasn't exactly unaffected by the heat, either, and she didn't think the way his muscles tensed had anything to do with the air temperature. Their bodies steamed with anticipation.

"I think..." He cleared his throat. "I think we should go downstairs now."

"But I thought we should start an inventory list. Do something productive."

"I'll have someone on my staff make a list and you can check it. Later."

"So, now what? Dinner?" she asked remembering his statement that they'd have dinner then each other.

"Are you hungry?"

She shook her head.

"Still want that tour?"

She nodded.

"Where do you want to start?"

Without any coyness or hesitation she answered, "Your room."

It was all Beau could do to keep from throwing her over his shoulder and racing for the bedroom. With his few remaining shreds of restraint he picked up her jacket, opened the door and ushered her out of the attic to the enormous master bedroom. The instant he closed the door and turned to her, she was tugging his T-shirt out of his jeans.

"You're going to be the death of me, darlin'." He helped her yank the shirt over his head.

"But what a way to go," they said in unison, then laughed.

Slowly Lily's laughter faded as she leaned forward and he felt her capture a tiny drop of sweat from the base of his throat. When she lifted her head, her eyes were closed.

She licked her lips.

And Beau went over the edge.

After that he was barely conscious of taking off his clothes or hers. Or carrying her to the bed. And only vaguely aware of pausing to reach for one of the foil-wrapped packets in a drawer beside the bed. All he knew for sure was that he couldn't think, couldn't breathe until he was inside her, buried so deep it was impossible to know where one person ended and the other began. And then he was and nothing else mattered.

"Lily...oh, Lily."

A shuddering climax hit her almost as soon as he entered her. She screamed her satisfaction, her hands clutching the sheets.

"That's it, darlin'. That's it." He drove her up again, slowing when she neared the peak. Then he did it again and again, until she was bucking beneath him, straining for release.

"Please, Beau...oh please."

"You're so greedy, I love that," he said, clinging to the very last of his own control. "So beautiful." He cupped her breasts, bent to kiss them.

At the first stroke of his tongue she shattered with pleasure. As he felt her body tremble with sweet satisfaction, he followed, pouring himself into her until he was drained, spent.

And happier than he could ever remember.

5

THE OLD-FASHIONED GLIDER at one end of the Matthews front porch creaked in protest as it slowly swung back and forth. Lily didn't notice. Her mind was across town as it always was these days. If she wasn't with Beau, she was thinking about him. Every day that passed he became more and more important to her. And every day she looked forward to the next.

The week or so he'd planned on staying in Rosemont had turned into three. And they were the happiest days Lily had ever known. Part of her time was spent in the library, part working on the Stuart mansion project and the rest was spent in Beau's arms and his bed. She was well aware of the dangers involved in her juggling act, but the payoff was worth it. The more she was with Beau, the more she wanted to be with him. It was as though time away from him held little meaning. Only when they were together did she feel alive, complete. Funny, she thought. How could she ever go back to the kind of life she lived before Beau came along?

She tried not to allow the questions concerning her

future to cloud her present happiness, but it was hard. Particularly when she knew her time with Beau was probably running short. It had to be. How long could she expect a man of his caliber to stay in a town too small and narrow-minded for his cosmopolitan tastes? They hadn't talked about when he was leaving since that first night she'd come to his house. A week or so he'd told her, just long enough to clear up Rowland Stuart's estate. Now the time had exceeded almost three weeks and each day she tried not to ask herself if today would be the day he decided to leave.

Not that he spent every waking moment in Rosemont. He'd spent a morning and a couple of afternoons in Richmond, but each time he'd been back in time to see her. She'd told herself a hundred times not to read too much into his attentive behavior, but she couldn't help herself. The uncertainty of when he would go led to a kind of desperation, an urgent need to make every minute, every second, count. Each night after they were together, she made dream deposits in her bank of memories. A hedge against the crash she knew was imminent. She savored each second in his arms, but she had also come to treasure equally the times when they were simply together.

She wouldn't, couldn't, in fact, deny that the sex was wonderful, nothing short of earth-shattering. But the moments they shared without sex were little dividends in her savings account of memories. They were full of surprises and always marvelous. She closed her eyes remembering the journal they'd found written around the turn of the century by Miss Prudence Green, a spinster lady related to the wife of one of Tobias Stuart's many sons. It seemed the woman felt it her duty to record in detail every infraction of the rather stiff Victorian moral code, such as the flash of an ankle, or a "lustful glance" and the shocking discovery that one of Tobias's granddaughters smoked. The journal was a real find not only for its meticulous documentation, but because of Miss Prudence's colorful commentary ranging from amusing to downright funny in places. She and Beau had read aloud to each other, laughing and joking about the changes in morals over the years. And somehow they had slipped into a rather bawdy question and answer session about how Miss Prudence might respond to modern changes such as women's lib, the sexual revolution and househusbands.

Lily smiled to herself remembering how they had entertained themselves for over an hour. It had been such fun. Silly, unconscious fun. The kind two people in a real relationship might share. And even though she knew it was dangerous to think about a real relationship with Beau, moments like sharing Miss Prudence's journal made her question her goal. What if this wonderful sexual fantasy turned into something more? What if she fell in love with Beau?

A niggling voice inside of her asked, What if she was already falling?

"Lily?"

She opened her eyes and found her mother standing a few feet away.

"You looked so peaceful, I thought you might have fallen asleep and were dreaming. A very pleasant dream from the look on your face."

"No, I wasn't asleep, just relaxing."

Amelia Matthews sat beside her daughter on the glider. "You've been working so hard lately it wouldn't surprise me if you had nodded off. This project of preserving the old Stuart place is important to you, isn't it?"

It was the first time her mother had mentioned the project since the night Lily had informed both her mother and aunt that she was committed to the restoration regardless of their opinions. Frankly she was relieved that her mother had brought up the subject on her own. "Yes, it's very important."

Amelia sighed. "I suppose you're still upset with me for opposing your participation."

"No."

"Well, to be honest I was extremely opposed in the beginning, but when I see how you've thrown your whole heart into the work and research, and, well..."

"Well, what?"

"I owe you an apology. It's not always easy for a parent to see their child as an adult. We tend to want to keep our babies, babies, you know?" She patted Lily's hand. "Anyway, I'm sorry I didn't trust your judgment."

"Thanks. I expected Aunt Pauline to take a hard line where Beau was concerned, but I hoped you would come to understand, and you did."

Amelia smiled. "Eventually."

Lily kissed her mother on the cheek. "That's what counts."

"I just wish…"

"What?"

"Oh, I don't know. Sometimes I feel as if I've let you down."

"How can you say that? You've never let me down."

"Of course I have. All parents disappoint their children just like children disappoint their parents. That's human nature. No, I meant that over the years I'm afraid my own need for privacy has been a terrible price for you to pay."

"I understand."

"I know you do and I want to thank you for that, and for following your own conscience. This project with Mr. Stuart is your way of standing up for our family, tainted though it may be, isn't it?"

"I suppose," Lily admitted. "But—"

"It's all right, dear." Amelia patted her hand, then took a deep breath and smiled. "So, are you and Mr. Stuart working tonight?"

"I think so," Lily said, going along with the change of subject. "He had some appointments in Richmond and said he would call when he got back. There's still so much to be done, cataloging, numbering, deciding which items will be displayed and how. It's a bigger job than I ever dreamed."

"But it's exciting, isn't it? It must be. I've never seen you so happy, so eager, almost glowing with anticipation."

Lily wanted to cry. She and her mother had always been so close that not being able to share with her now was painful. Maybe if she just talked about how kind Beau was, how much she enjoyed his company, maybe...

At that moment a car pulled into the driveway and stopped. Both women looked up and, to their mutual shock, Beau got out of the car.

Lily jumped to her feet, fear clutching her heart. Something was wrong. Her first thought was that he'd broken his promise, but even as the thought formed she discounted it. There was no basis for her fear and deep in her heart she knew it. If he'd wanted to blow the whistle on her he could have done it days ago. Besides, she had trusted him from the beginning; there was no reason to stop now. "Beau, I'm surprised to see you here."

Smiling, he stepped onto the porch. "Good evening, Lily." Then he turned to her mother. "And you must be Lily's mother."

"Oh, that's right," Lily said, feeling more awkward by the minute, not because she was concerned about what he would say, but because of the absurdity of having to introduce a man she had been totally intimate with to her mother for the first time. "You two haven't met. Mom, this is Beau Stuart. Beau, this is my mother, Amelia Matthews."

They shook hands. "It's a real pleasure to meet you, Ms. Matthews, and I hope you'll forgive my deplorable disregard for manners by coming here without even calling. Please believe me when I tell you that I was raised better, but it's very important that I speak with Lily, and I'm in a real time crunch."

"You're forgiven, Mr. Stuart. And may I say how pleased I am to make your acquaintance, and very pleased about your donating your house."

"Well, to be honest, Ms. Matthews, I don't feel as if the house is mine. I never spent much time there or felt like it was a home."

"I *did* spend a lot of time in that house when I was a little girl, but you're right. It never felt like a home. In fact, it always frightened me a little."

Beau grinned. "Well, that's a relief. I gotta tell you I've hung back from even telephoning Lily at her home because I wasn't sure how you felt about the project or me."

"I was hesitant, at first, but now the project has my wholehearted approval."

"Only the project? I was hoping you wouldn't believe everything you've probably heard about me."

Amelia Matthews blinked. "Oh, my," she said. "Lily told me you were...up-front I believe is the word she used, but now I understand what she meant. Are you always so forthright?"

"Always, ma'am. Particularly with women."

Lily thought she caught the beginnings of a grin on her mother's lips and breathed a sigh of relief. Oh, if only her mother could get to know Beau as she had.

"That's a very enlightened point of view, Mr. Stuart," Amelia said.

"Well, now, I can't say it's purely altruistic. I've discovered that good-looking women with brains won't give a chauvinist the time of day."

"Very perceptive."

"Coming from a smart, attractive lady, I'll take that as a compliment, ma'am."

Amelia's hint of a grin became a full-fledged, and very warm, smile. "As pleasant as this has been, I don't think you came to flatter me, so I'll let you and Lily conduct your business." She walked to the front door, stopped and turned back to him. "After meeting you, Mr. Stuart, I do believe at least one thing I've heard about you."

"And that would be...?"

"You *are* a smooth-talker, and I suspect a bit of a rogue." Then she went inside.

Beau looked at Lily. "Think I made a good impression?"

"Possibly, but I'm more concerned with why you needed to speak with me and this time crunch you mentioned."

"Will you walk me to my car?"

"Of course, but I don't—"

"Just walk with me," he insisted.

When they reached his car and he opened the door, a sudden chill danced down her spine. He was going away. She knew it, felt it. And it hurt more than she could ever have imagined.

With the open door between them he rested his right forearm on the top and said, "I have to leave. The manager of my New Orleans office walked out unexpectedly and the whole place is in turmoil. If I don't get down there and stomp out a few fires no telling where it will end. I just wanted you to know—"

"You don't owe me any explanations." Lily rushed to head him off. Suddenly the thought of him saying goodbye was unbearable, but there was nothing she could do about it except hang on to her dignity, when she wanted to beg him to stay. The force of her wanting, needing him, to stay hit her like a plunge into an icy ocean. She couldn't let him see...he couldn't know. "I mean, it's not like we didn't both know this day would come. No strings—"

"Lily."

"No regrets, remember? It was fun while it lasted, but—"

"Lily."

"I understand and, after all, you—"

"I was experienced, available and temporary, right?"

Suddenly she realized her own words were now a bitter pill to swallow. She looked away. He couldn't see her tears; it would ruin everything. "Right."

"Wrong."

Her gaze shot to his. "But I—"

"Talk too much. I am leaving, but I'll be back day after tomorrow." He leaned over the door still separating them. "You can't get rid of me that easy."

She smiled. "Oh, Beau, I..." She wanted to throw her arms around his neck and smother him with kisses.

"Better stop looking at me like that," he said, grinning.

Could he see the need in her eyes? "Like what?"

"Like you wanted to strip me naked and make love to me."

Relief sighed from her body. "I was just wishing I could kiss you goodbye."

"I was just thinking about doing a lot more than kissing, but we don't have time."

"That's a shame."

"You're telling me. Why do you think I deliberately put this door between us? If this barrier wasn't here..."

"What?" she teased, her relief giving her enough security again to be daring despite standing in the middle of her driveway in broad daylight. "What would you do if the barrier was gone?"

He laughed through his teeth. "You're bad, you know that?"

"That's not what you said last night."

For the benefit of anyone watching, he smiled, nodding as if they were having a normal conversation. "If your mother and probably half the neighborhood weren't peering through their curtains at us right this minute wondering what we're saying, I'd show you what bad really is."

"Is that a promise?"

His eyes glinted with the blue-white fire she now recognized and appreciated. "Just wait until I get back."

Lily smiled. "Very well, Mr. Stuart," she said loud enough for at least the next door neighbor to hear. "Let me know when you return and we'll pick up the project where we left off."

"Oh, absolutely, Miss Matthews. I'm eager to resume our work."

When he got into the car and closed the door he said in a low voice, "I'll be back as fast as I can."

"Hurry," she whispered.

A second later Lily waved as he drove off. She

wanted to stand and watch until his car disappeared from sight, but didn't dare. She also wanted to cry. She did neither. Instead, she turned and walked into the house at a normal pace as if it was a casual parting between business acquaintances. No one could even suspect this day was different from any other. It was, of course. She'd realized it the moment Beau announced he was leaving. No, before, actually. How ironic, she thought. When he'd driven up to the house, she'd been afraid he'd betrayed her and, in reality, she'd betrayed herself.

While her intellect had always known he would leave, her emotions didn't want to face that reality. And no matter how many times she'd told herself not to get involved, she had. What a fool she'd been to think she could give her body to a man night after night and keep her heart separate. And an even bigger fool to think she could avoid a broken heart.

Lily paused for a moment at the front door. No, this day certainly wasn't like any other in her twenty-four and a half years. Maybe she should circle it in red on her calendar.

After all, it wasn't every day a woman realized she was in love.

BEAU CHECKED HIS WATCH for what felt like the tenth time in as many minutes. The plane that would carry him back to Virginia was almost an hour late due to storms in the Southwest. He wouldn't make it back to Rosemont until after midnight. Which meant he wouldn't have Lily all to himself until the following night. He wasn't sure he could wait that long. Scarcely more than twenty-four hours had passed since he'd seen her and he was practically pawing at the ground like a stallion in rut.

This wasn't like him. In fact, that could be said about a lot of things he'd done over the past three weeks. He was accustomed to doing business on the run. His house in Richmond was home base, but he was rarely there for more than a few weeks at a time. He owned a cabin just outside of Breckenridge, Colorado, and an apartment in New Orleans, but he spent very little time at either place. Yet he'd spent almost three weeks in a town he'd couldn't tolerate, in a house he hated. Funny, he thought. He had no feelings one way or the other about any of the houses he owned but just the thought of the Stuart mansion triggered a strong emotional response.

The move to donate the property had been a wise one. He didn't regret it, particularly since it gave him the opportunity to spend time with Lily. But something had happened to him as the two of them pored over stacks of old journals and sepia-toned pictures. For the first time he felt connected to the man that fathered him. Not necessarily love, but a connection, nonetheless. Something he never expected or even wanted. But Lily had made him understand that, even though he'd never been recognized as a "legitimate" Stuart, he was one, and should be proud of his heritage. He smiled remembering the day she'd practically lectured him like one of the students that regularly visited her library. She'd gotten up a real head of steam over the whole thing to the point of shaking her finger at him with a couple of "you should be ashamed" and "you have a right to take pride in your ancestry, no matter which side of the blanket you were born on."

The whole episode had ended with him meekly agreeing right before he grabbed her, kissed and tickled her into a fit of laughing. That afternoon had turned out to be long, lusty and just about the most satisfying he could ever remember. And he wanted another just like it. A lot more just like it. And not just because of the sex. He wanted more of Lily. Lecturing, laughing, smiling, in bed and out, he wanted to be with her.

Just her.

The admission couldn't have stunned him more if a total stranger had walked up and socked him in the jaw. He sat down in the nearest chair.

He'd never thought in terms of just one woman before. Ever. In fact, he'd always made it a point not to, usually dating two or three women at one time. Yet, he'd hardly given a thought to any woman other than Lily since that first night she'd come to him with her "plan." What was happening to him? Yes, Lily was sweet, sexy and totally engaging, but she wasn't for him any more than he was for her. This was ridiculous. He wasn't looking for just one woman and if he had been, Lily couldn't be the one. And even if she was, it would never work. They came from different backgrounds and didn't want the same—

Listen to yourself, he thought. So Lily was the hottest woman he'd known in many years. So what? Sure he wanted to be with her. Why not? That didn't mean he'd gone off the deep end about her, and it sure as hell didn't mean he wanted to be tied to just one woman. Of course not. They were great together in bed, and out of it, she was good company. Nothing more. No need to get excited about the idea of a deeper relationship with Lily. Satisfied that his momentary panic attack had not only passed, but was unjustified to begin with, he headed for the airline desk to check on his flight. It didn't register that he'd consciously used two words previously considered part of a foreign language where his love life was concerned.

Deep and relationship.

"HELLO," LILY SAID, catching the phone in her office on the third ring.

"What are you doing at the library this late?"

At the sound of Beau's voice her heartbeat tripled. "Catching up on some work," she said, hoping her voice didn't sound breathy.

"How's everything going?"

"Oh, just fine." Except that she'd missed him in a way she didn't think was possible to miss another human being. Except that she'd laid awake two nights thinking about him and, when she'd finally fallen asleep, had dreamed about him. "With the help of a stack of old firearms reference books I managed to catalog the rest of the antique guns we found in the cellar."

"Great."

"I'm not sure how great since I was up all last night working on them."

"All night?"

"Pretty much. Until four this morning." The inane conversation was a poor substitute for being in his arms.

"So, you're tired?"

She was tired and had been ever since he left, but something in the tone of his voice prompted her to answer with a question of her own. "Where are you?"

"I just passed the Rosemont city limits sign and you didn't answer my question."

She smiled, practically dancing in place with excitement. "Not that tired."

"How soon can you—"

"Give me an hour to close up and freshen up then I'll—"

"Too long. I'll take you just like you are."

"Remember you said that."

"Twenty minutes?"

"Make it fifteen."

When she hung up the phone she wondered how she would feel when she saw him again now that she'd fallen in love with him. Funny, she thought, she'd always expected the moment she knew she was in love to be a glorious, the-earth-stood-still kind of moment. But it hadn't been that way at all. Instead she'd been filled with a quiet joy, and peace. It wasn't as shocking as she'd expected, but then, she realized she'd been in love with Beau from the first moment she met him. No, actually she'd been in love with the idea of him much longer. Possibly all her life.

WHEN LILY PULLED into the driveway of the Stuart mansion, the front door opened and Beau stepped outside. She parked, got out, then just stood there staring at him. As anxious as she'd been to see him, now she hesitated. And even though she couldn't tell him how she felt, she feared he might see it in her eyes. "Hi," she said.

"Hi, yourself." When she didn't move he asked, "You gonna stand there all night?"

This was insane, she thought, her hesitation finally giving way to the pure joy of seeing him again. Besides, she'd come this far on sheer determination, no point in wimping out now. "No," she finally said, the fatigue she'd felt earlier melting away. She walked straight into his arms.

"God, you feel good," he breathed against her hair, holding her tight.

"So do you."

"I've got to kiss you." He lifted her off the ground, carried her inside and was doing just that before the door closed. He kissed her hard. Deep. Long and passionate. Every way he'd been wanting to kiss her for the past two days.

"How long can you stay?" he rasped between fevered kisses.

"An hour. Maybe more."

"Not long enough. Not nearly long enough."

"I know."

"Upstairs," he said. "Come with me."

She didn't need to respond. They both wanted the same thing, needed the same thing. Arms wrapped around each other's waists, they climbed the stairs.

Once inside his room he pulled her into his arms and proceeded to kiss her senseless. He devoured her mouth then rained kisses over her face and neck. He nibbled her lips, teased her tongue, then kissed her again, making love to her mouth.

Lily couldn't get close enough, couldn't touch him enough. And everywhere he touched her he left trails of heat. Hot, greedy streamers of need spiraled through her. "Beau," she whispered, feeling as if she were melting from the inside out. "Beau—"

He cupped her breasts in his hands, and she forgot what she wanted to say, instead crying out with pleasure when he rubbed her hardened nipples through her blouse. Then he plunged his tongue into her mouth and her knees went weak. Whether to hold on or do some sensual assaulting of her own, she grabbed the waist of his jeans, slipping her fingers between denim and flesh.

He moaned and the weakness disappeared. Power surged through her knowing that just her touch could make him moan. Empowered, she boldly unsnapped his jeans, yanked the zipper down and shoved her hands under the waistband of his underwear and over his buttocks.

This time he groaned, pulling her against him, almost crushing her to him. The fierce embrace lasted only seconds, then surprisingly, he backed away.

"Where are you go—"

"Just..." Leaning forward, he put his hands on his thighs. "Just give me a minute, darlin', or that's about how long this will last."

"Come back here so I can kiss you."

He wagged his finger at her. "You're not helping."

She started unbuttoning her blouse. "I will."

"Lily, you don't seem to understand—"

"Yes, I do."

"No, if I don't get some control we won't make it to the bed. I'll take you right here, right now and that's not how I wanted it."

She shrugged out of the blouse and sent it sailing into a nearby chair. "Too bad."

"Have some pity. I'm barely hanging on here. I might not be able to last long enough—"

"I don't care."

"You say that now."

"Hmm." She removed her bra.

"Lily, wait—"

"No," she insisted, and shimmied out of her jeans. "No more waiting."

It was the shimmy that did it. He reached for her, knowing he couldn't stop now if the world was ending. Two seconds later he was as naked as she and they made it to the bed. But only just. He paused long enough to sheathe himself in one of the condoms he kept in a nightstand beside the bed, before he drove into her. She came instantly and the last thin shred of his control snapped. He stroked hard once, twice and then with an almost primeval groan of possession, he climaxed.

Moments later they lay entangled in each other's arms, breathing hard, their bodies damp. Beau kissed her closed eyelids, expecting hardly more than a sigh of satisfaction. He got it, but when she opened her eyes he saw passion still blazing in their depths. Hunger. Raw hunger. And it matched his own. A deep, mind-robbing hunger he'd never known. Too powerful to fight. She moaned, squirming beneath him, needing again. He withdrew, pulled on a fresh condom and slipped back inside her.

He was able to hold back this time, able to draw out her pleasure and his. Putting both hands beneath her fanny he lifted her, filling her completely, only to withdraw and slowly fill her again. He did it over and over. Hard and deep. Hot and greedy. Slow and fast. Until she was wild again, her nails digging into his shoulders, her hips rotating to the eternally primitive beat. He watched as she shuddered through one release and began the climb to another. Then he rolled to his back, taking her with him. Her eyes flew open then drifted closed as he put his hands on her hips and coaxed her to move, giving her control. She took it and him. All of him. And this time they came together, flying over the edge of the world into a dark, sweet oblivion.

Later, after Lily had showered and dressed, Beau walked her to the door.

"I want a night," he said. "A whole night. Can you arrange it?"

"I think so. Yes."

"Good." He slipped his arms around her, drew her to him. "Call me greedy, but there's never enough time with you."

"I know. I feel the same way."

"Then you'll work it out to spend a whole night? We can go to Richmond. The best hotel. Whatever you want."

"I want what we had tonight. Right here in your room."

Surprised, but pleased, Beau kissed her lightly on the mouth. "Your wish is my command."

She gave him a sexy little grin. "You may be sorry you said that."

"Oh, I hope so." He kissed her again. "I surely hope so, darlin'."

6

SEATED AT THE KITCHEN table, Lily and Amelia exchanged glances when the back door opened, then slammed shut. Without turning around in her chair, Amelia said, "Good morning, Pauline. Would you like some coffee?"

"What I would like," Pauline said, waving that morning's edition of the *Rosemont Register* in her hand, "is an explanation from my niece."

Lily looked up. "About what, Aunt Pauline?"

"About this." She snapped open the newspaper and plopped it down on the table.

"Yes, that situation in Kosovo is getting worse by the—"

"Not that. This." Pauline's finger tapped the headline of one of the columns. "Your Mr. Stuart is giving with one hand and taking with the other."

Lily picked up the paper, quickly scanning the article. She looked at her aunt. "This is just talking about Stuart Electronics."

"What about them?" Amelia asked.

Pauline put her hands on her hips. "The company may be closing. That's what."

How To Play:

No Risk!

1. With a coin, carefully scratch off the 3 gold areas on your Lucky Carnival Wheel. By doing so you have qualified to receive everything revealed — 2 FREE books and a surprise gift — ABSOLUTELY FREE!

2. Send back this card and you'll receive brand-new Harlequin Temptation® novels. These books have a cover price of $3.99 each in the U.S. and $4.50 each in Canada, but they are yours TOTALLY FREE!

3. There's no catch! You're under no obligation to buy anything. We charge nothing — ZERO — for your first shipment. And you don't have to make any minimum number of purchases — not even one!

4. The fact is thousands of readers enjoy receiving books by mail from the Harlequin Reader Service®. They enjoy the convenience of home delivery—they like getting the best new novels at discount prices, BEFORE they're available in stores...and they love their *Heart to Heart* subscriber newsletter featuring author news, horoscopes, recipes, book reviews and much more!

No Cost!

5. We hope that after receiving your free books you'll want to remain a subscriber. But the choice is yours — to continue or cancel, anytime at all! So why not take us up on our invitation, with no risk of any kind. You'll be glad you did.

LUCKY Carnival Wheel

Find Out Instantly The Gifts You Get Absolutely FREE!

Scratch-off Game →

Scratch off **ALL 3** Gold areas

YES!

I have scratched off the 3 Gold Areas above. Please send me the 2 FREE books and gift for which I qualify! I understand I am under no obligation to purchase any books, as explained on the back and on the opposite page.

342 HDL CY44

142 HDL CY4U

NAME   (PLEASE PRINT CLEARLY)

ADDRESS

APT.#   CITY

STATE/PROV.   ZIP/POSTAL CODE

(H-T-04/00)

► DETACH AND MAIL CARD TODAY!

The Harlequin Reader Service® — Here's how it works:

Accepting your 2 free books and gift places you under no obligation to buy anything. You may keep the books and gift and return the shipping statement marked "cancel." If you do not cancel, about a month later we'll send you 4 additional novels and bill you just $3.34 each in the U.S., or $3.80 each in Canada, plus 25¢ delivery per book and applicable taxes if any.* That's the complete price and — compared to cover prices of $3.99 each in the U.S. and $4.50 each in Canada — it's quite a bargain! You may cancel at any time, but if you choose to continue, every month we'll send you 4 more books, which you may either purchase at the discount price or return to us and cancel your subscription.

*Terms and prices subject to change without notice. Sales tax applicable in N.Y. Canadian residents will be charged applicable provincial taxes and GST.

If offer card is missing write to: Harlequin Reader Service, 3010 Walden Ave., P.O. Box 1867, Buffalo, NY 14240-1867

BUSINESS REPLY MAIL
FIRST-CLASS MAIL   PERMIT NO. 717   BUFFALO, NY

POSTAGE WILL BE PAID BY ADDRESSEE

HARLEQUIN READER SERVICE
3010 WALDEN AVE
PO BOX 1867
BUFFALO NY 14240-9952

NO POSTAGE
NECESSARY
IF MAILED
IN THE
UNITED STATES

Amelia took the paper from Lily. "Oh, no."

"Oh, yes. What do you think of Beau Stuart now? Didn't I tell you he didn't care one whit for the people in this town? He's probably laughing up the sleeve of one of his thousand-dollar suits right this minute."

"He doesn't wear thousand-dollar suits," Lily informed her.

"Well, you can bet he's laughing. Half the people in this town are employed by Stuart Electronics and they're all going to be out of a job."

"There's nothing in this article that says the plant is definitely closing," Amelia said. "It states that the company is considering several options including revamping management."

"That's corporate double-talk for cutbacks and layoffs."

Amelia shook her head. "Oh, I hope not. He seemed like a perfectly nice person when I met him a few days ago."

"He is nice, Mother," Lily assured her.

"Amelia Jackson Matthews, I'm appalled at your attitude. You're beginning to sound like your daughter."

"Now, Pauline."

"Well, it's true. The man donates a house and she thinks he's some kind of wonderful do-gooder with no ulterior motives. And I tell you he wants to get even with the town for snubbing him as a kid. She needs to remember who she is. There's been enough talk as it is.''

"She is right here. I'd appreciate it if you didn't talk about me in the third person, Aunt Pauline. And for your information, Beau isn't out for revenge, though Lord knows he'd be justified. And as for remembering who I am, it's pretty damned hard to forget. Even if I tried, I'm sure you'd be right here to jog my memory.''

Pauline's mouth dropped open. "You see what I mean? I wouldn't stand for that kind of language if I were you, Amelia.''

"Lily, I think Aunt Pauline is only trying to point out that—"

"That we Matthews have to be careful, right?" She got up from the table, trembling with a combination of frustration and anger. "We can't afford even a whiff of scandal..." At the stricken look on her mother's face, Lily was instantly ashamed. "Oh, Mom. I'm sorry.''

"As you should be," Pauline directed. "And since you seem to be on good enough terms with Mr. Stuart to defend him, I suggest that you do your best to find out exactly what he intends to do about the factory.''

"Pauline," her sister-in-law cautioned, "you can't expect Lily to spy on the man.''

"No," Lily said. "I won't spy, but I will ask him.''

"You don't expect him to tell you the truth, do you?" Pauline huffed.

"Yes, I do. And he will."

"Now, Lily. Don't be upset with Aunt Pauline. She's only thinking of our reputation."

Lily wanted to scream "to hell with my reputation," but of course, she didn't. Throwing a temper fit wouldn't do anything but make the situation worse. "I'm not upset," she lied, taking a deep breath. "But I can't talk about this anymore. I'll be late for work as it is."

Pauline drew herself up, tilted her chin in the air. "Are you going to see—"

"No, I'm not seeing Beau tonight." Another lie, but she was struggling not to completely lose her patience with her well-meaning, but annoying aunt. She made a point of turning away from Pauline and speaking directly to her mother. "As a matter of fact, I'm spending the night with Connie in Richmond. We're going to the opening of a new art gallery, then tomorrow morning we're going to a brunch sponsored by her book club. I should be home around one o'clock."

"That's fine, dear. I think you should have a good time once in a while."

"You mean you aren't going to pore over journals and date furniture with Mr. Stuart? I can't believe you'd give up time on your precious project for fun," Pauline said.

Lily rose from the table. "It's the weekend, Aunt Pauline. I'm entitled to a little fun. But I promise you one thing. The next time I see Beau, I'll ask him about his plans for the microchip plant, even though it's none of my business. There, satisfied?" Without waiting for an answer she turned on her heels and left the kitchen.

Still fuming ten minutes later as she walked to work, she thought about the first night she'd gone to the Stuart mansion. Beau had assumed she'd come on behalf of the city to ask his intentions concerning the plant. But a microchip plant had been the furthest thing from her mind, and to be honest she hadn't given it another thought since then. Until today. Still, regardless of the slant of the newspaper article, she didn't believe Beau had just been biding his time, waiting to close the plant. There was no way she could have been so close to him and misjudged his character to that extent. He wasn't cold and calculating the way a lot of people in town thought, including Aunt Pauline. For probably the dozenth time she wished they knew the Beau Stuart she knew. Yes, he was a no-nonsense businessman, but he wasn't heartless. Dammit, they had no right to judge him the way they had. She was so angry she wanted to tell them they were all acting like idiots.

Lily sighed, slowing her pace. Simmer down, she told herself. She was justified in directing only part of her anger toward the townspeople. The rest of it, she realized, belonged to her. Even knowing self-recriminations served no purpose, she berated herself for becoming emotionally involved with Beau.

How could she have fallen for him? How could she have been so arrogant as to think she had covered all the bases with her plan? This was certainly one base she hadn't counted on, and she wasn't exactly sure how to handle it. Of course, she wouldn't tell Beau. She wouldn't tell anyone. Ever. Aunt Pauline would be horrified. Her mother would be hurt and disappointed. And Beau probably wouldn't even believe her. Not after the way she'd begun their relationship. He'd bargained for sex, not a lovesick...

Lovesick? Is that what she was? She'd felt so... wrung-out for the past several days, physically and emotionally, but due to the hours she'd put in on the project she hadn't given it a lot of concern. Love was supposed to make you feel good, wasn't it? And wasn't it supposed to make you hopeful, eager for the future.

The only time she felt good was with Beau.

And her future looked painfully empty without him.

Lily stopped walking as an overwhelming feeling of foreboding came over her. Suddenly she felt as if her whole life was on the cusp of a dramatic change. It could only mean one thing.

Beau would soon be gone.

Lily shuddered, knowing that her instincts were

undoubtedly right on. Tonight would probably be the only time they would ever spend the night together. It might even be the last time they were together, period. Even if that weren't the case, how much time could she possibly have left? A day? Three? Four? And in the end, did the number of days even matter? The results would be the same. Beau would be gone and she would be alone with nothing but memories. Suddenly nothing else mattered but tonight. She wanted every minute, every second to be memorable. They would laugh, tease and make hot, exquisite love. Tonight would be perfect. She would keep her promise to Aunt Pauline, but that's where all thoughts of anyone but herself and Beau would end. After that, the outside world wouldn't exist.

As Beau came down the wide stairway to the foyer he smiled, well pleased with himself. He'd gone to some trouble to recreate the first night Lily came to him. Dinner was waiting in the library. The wine was chilling while fireplace and candles glowed. Soft music was playing. He'd even remembered the flowers, only he'd increased their presence. An arrangement of lilies, twice the size of the first one, was on the entry table. Not only were there violets on the table set for two, but decorative nosegays dotted the library as well. The only thing different, and it was a big difference, was the master bedroom upstairs.

There, too, a fire and candles glowed. And a single long-stemmed rose rested on one pillow. He and Lily had never gotten to the bedroom that first night, but they would tonight and he wanted to make it as special as he could.

And not just for Lily.

He'd done some thinking since he got back from New Orleans, or more accurately since the first night he'd returned. When he'd opened the door and had seen her standing in his driveway something strange had happened. It hadn't been his body that reacted immediately.

It had been his heart.

It had slowly tightened to the point that he'd feared it might burst with the pure joy of seeing her again.

A few seconds later his body had indeed responded in the way he'd expected and he'd pushed that first reaction from his mind, still trying to convince himself lust was all that was between them. But later, after Lily had gone, he'd started to think about that reaction and what it meant. He'd been awake most of the night thinking about it. At first he denied feeling more than lust, just as he had in the airport, but denial didn't work anymore. She'd become too important to him for a mere casual fling. Then he'd tried to analyze his feelings. That didn't work, either. How does a man make sense out of emotions for years he'd insisted were senseless?

He'd truly loved only one person in his life—his mother.

Losing her was the most painful thing he'd ever experienced and, somewhere along the line, he'd decided that if he didn't love, he didn't hurt. Even though he'd told himself he would marry and have a family someday, a part of him never really believed it. The truth was he hadn't felt this close to anyone since his mother died and he wasn't sure he liked it. So, after hours of trying to look at the problem objectively and from every angle, he'd come to several conclusions.

Whatever he felt for Lily was stronger than he'd thought, and it wasn't getting any weaker.

Even though he hadn't wanted a relationship, he had one now, and it wasn't as confining as he'd expected.

And last, but not least, no other woman had ever made him question what he wanted, just as no other woman had ever made him feel as Lily did.

As for defining "love," he wasn't ready to take that step, but he had a hunch he was closer to the brink than he wanted to admit.

Maybe it was just as well he was going away on business again. He'd been ignoring the situation with the plant here in Rosemont and if today's newspaper was an accurate barometer, the natives were getting restless. He had to make some decisions, but to do that, first he had to lock himself up with T.J.

and his advisers for at least a couple of days of serious brainstorming. And a few days away from Lily might be just what he needed. Being with her crowded out everything else. Abstinence might help him clear his head. Still, he dreaded leaving, dreaded telling her he was going. That was another reason he wanted tonight to be perfect for both of them.

The doorbell chimed and he walked to the door. When he opened it Lily stood on the other side dressed in slacks and a tailored blouse. A small suitcase rested beside her feet.

"Good evening, sir. I'm working my way through college selling door-to-door and I was wondering if I could interest you in some items?"

Grinning, he cleared his throat and tried to look put-off. "No, salesman," he told her.

"Salesperson," she corrected him. "Now, you look like a man of discerning taste, and I believe I could show you something you'd want."

He eyed the suitcase. "In that little bag, I suppose."

"Absolutely."

"Animal, vegetable or mineral."

"Oh, animal. Definitely, animal."

"Then, by all means, come right in."

Lily swept through the door and right into his arms. "You're in a playful mood," he said, kissing her several times before releasing her to pick up her bag and close the door.

"You ain't seen nothing yet," she promised, then upon seeing the display of lilies exclaimed, "Oh, how lovely."

"They don't hold a candle to you." Then he took her hand. "C'mon, dinner's waiting."

She stopped when she saw the library. "Oh, Beau," she said, moved to see his efforts to duplicate their first night. "This is so sweet."

"Glad you like it." He stepped behind her, slipped his arms around her waist and kissed her neck. "How about some wine?"

Lily laughed. "You wouldn't be thinking of plying me with drink so you could take advantage of me, would you?"

"Would it work?"

"Forget it. You don't need the wine."

"You keep looking at me like that and I'll need more than wine to make it through the night. Let's have some food to fortify us."

"You went to so much trouble that I hate to tell you I'm not all that hungry."

"Well, you're going to eat anyway. I swear, I think you've lost a pound or two."

"Flatterer."

He poured two glasses of wine and handed her one. "You don't need to lose weight. But you do need to stop working so hard. Seriously, Lily, you look tired."

"Don't be silly. Anytime I don't get my full eight

hours it shows on my face. I'd hoped the candlelight would hide it."

"It's still a beautiful face." He kissed her gently on the lips. "But I want to see these cheeks rosy and these eyes sparkling when I get back—"

"Back?"

"Damn. Sorry, I intended to tell you, but not quite like that. I have to go away for a few days, Lily. I'll be in Richmond all day tomorrow, then tomorrow night I fly to the West Coast. It's business and I have to go."

His mention of business reminded her of her promise to Aunt Pauline. She wasn't thrilled about interjecting the topic into their evening, but better to get it out of the way. "I understand. Speaking of business, I suppose you've read today's *Rosemont Register*?"

"Yeah."

"Well, since we're sort of reliving our first night, do you remember that you thought I'd been sent here to get information about the plant."

"I remember."

"I didn't come for the city then and I'm not asking for them now, but..."

"But?"

"Not that this should concern you, but my aunt and my mother, mostly my aunt, are troubled by the article and concerned about the future of the plant. I promised her that I would ask you point-blank what you intended to do with it.''

''Sorry if that damned article caused you trouble at home, but the honest truth is I don't know. That's why I'm going to the coast to meet with my advisers and investors.''

''Are you thinking about closing the plant?''

''It's an option,'' he admitted. ''But certainly not my first choice. I wish I could send you back to your aunt with more, but I just won't have it until I get back. Will that do?''

''I guess it will have to.''

''I know I'm not exactly welcomed with open arms. Are you caught in the middle?''

''Not really. As I've told you before, they both know how I feel. Do you mind if I tell them what you've told me? I mean, this meeting isn't a secret, is it?''

''Help yourself. Tell anyone that asks.''

''Thanks, Beau.''

He came to her, touched her cheek with his hand. ''Thanks for not assuming the worst.''

''You're very welcome. Now can we forget about plants and aunts and concentrate on each other?''

''My pleasure, darlin'. Wanna start by telling me what you've got in your little bag?''

''I'll do better than that. I'll show you.'' When he took her in his arms, she added, ''After dinner.''

''Oh, I see. Torture, huh?''

"Like I said, 'you ain't seen nothing yet.'"

Their dinner was a wonderful, relaxing prelude to what they both knew would be a fantastic night. The food was delicious and Lily couldn't resist teasing him about slaving away over a hot stove all day just to impress her.

"Did it work?" he asked, giving her one of those slow, lazy grins she loved so much.

"When I was a little girl my mother always taught me to be appreciative of special efforts."

They had stretched out on the floor in front of the fireplace to enjoy their after-dinner drinks. Beau rolled over on his stomach, propped his chin in one hand and gazed up at her.

"I'll bet you were the perfect little girl, all ruffles and ribbons. No tomboy stuff for you."

"I was not," she lied.

He grinned. "Liar, liar, pants on fire. I can see you now, all neat as a pin, tight braids and freckles." He leaned closer. "Still got a few left. There're three on the bridge of your nose."

Lily's hand automatically went to that spot. She'd hated all her freckles, then and now. "How ungentlemanly of you to notice."

"I think they're cute."

"Cute? No woman past the age of twelve wants to be thought of as cute."

"Believe me, darlin', I don't think of you as a little girl. What else did your mother teach you?"

"Probably the same things your mother taught you. Stuff like, remember the three R's—respect for self, respect for others, responsibility for all of your actions."

"Better than reading, 'riting and 'rithmetic. What else?"

She leaned back on one elbow only because it brought her closer to him. "Hmm, let's see... Learn the rules, then break some."

"Like that one."

"I thought you would. Only in your case it would be break a lot. How about this one. Character is your destiny. Or, when you say 'I'm sorry,' look the person in the eye."

"Good advice. I knew I liked your mother."

"And then there're my personal favorites. Watch out for tall, smooth-talking men. And, don't trust a man who doesn't close his eyes when you kiss."

"Oh, now that sounds like a challenge." In a flash he caught her upper arm and dragged her to him. "I'd hate for you to think I'm not trustworthy." As he lowered his head to kiss her his eyes closed, but before they did she saw his gaze deepen and spark with heat.

One touch of his lips and playtime was over. This was what she'd been waiting for all night. But the kiss was too sweet and way too short. He drew back, got to his feet and helped her up.

"Not again. As tempting as you are, and as much

as I wanted tonight to remind you of our first night, I am not going to take you on the floor. We're going upstairs."

She put her hand on his cheek ever so gently as if to soothe him, then did a wicked about-face by running her finger along his bottom lip and slipping the tip inside.

He captured her hand. "Naughty, girl. Save it until we get upstairs." Then he kissed the tip of each finger before he tucked her hand in his and lead her from the room.

The first thing Lily saw when she walked into his room was the red rose on the pillow. She walked over, picked it up and inhaled its fragrance. "Lovely." She gazed up at him. "Very sweet and very thoughtful."

"I removed every thorn personally." He held up his right thumb. "See."

The spot where he'd been pricked was so tiny she had to look twice to find it, but it was the thought that counted. "My wounded hero," she cooed, bringing his thumb to her mouth. She kissed it, then drew it into her mouth and sucked.

His eyes widened, his body tensed and his breathing hardened along with the rest of his body. Without a word, he withdrew his hand and began pulling her blouse from the waistband of her slacks. Slowly he pushed each button through their holes with deliberate care. When it was done he slipped the blouse from her shoulders. Then, just as carefully, he unhooked the front closure of her bra and discarded it.

"You have the most beautiful skin." He put his hands at the base of her throat, sliding them over her shoulders, down her arms to her fingertips. Then he moved his hands to her waist and paused. He could feel her trembling with an anticipation that matched his own. "I want to see all of you," he said, unzipping her slacks. "Do you realize I've never seen all of you, all at once, in the light?"

"Or I, you." She helped by quickly stepping out of the slacks and kicking them aside. But when she reached for the lacy waistband of her panties, he stopped her.

"Let me."

He pushed the panties over her hips and down her legs, then she was naked.

"Now you," she said and duplicated his actions, just as slowly, just as deliberately, until they were both gloriously naked.

"C'mon." He took her hand and led her across the room to where an ornately carved cheval mirror stood. He put her in front of the mirror with him behind so they could both see. "Look at how beautiful you are."

Lily had never before stood so completely nude in front of a man. It was a little naughty...and thrilling. "This is downright decadent."

"It's downright erotic."

"It is, isn't it."

"Decadent, erotic—" he lifted her hair from her neck and kissed her bare shoulder "—delicious."

She closed her eyes and sighed. "Wonderful."

"Wonderful," he repeated, giving kisses to her other shoulder. "Sexy."

"Hmm." A sweet fire churned in the pit of her belly and thrummed through her blood. Her whole body vibrated with anticipation.

As before, he rested his hands at her neck then slid them down her shoulders to her fingertips then back up to her neck. Then he began a slow, steady, light massage, his fingers gently kneading her flesh. He stroked between her shoulder blades down to the curve of her spine, letting his fingers caress as well as massage. "I love the way your skin feels. Soft, warm. I love the way you smell. Like sunshine and a summer breeze." His hands continued their sensual massaging, over her shoulders, up to her nape, then down and around her rib cage to caress the underside of her breasts.

And when his thumbs began to stoke her soft fullness the vibrations sharpened, sang through her. She sighed again.

"Open your eyes," he said, his voice raw, husky with need. "See how sexy you are."

She did as he commanded, watching enthralled as his hands cupped her, kneaded her breasts. Instinctively she moved her arms to give him greater access.

"All I have to do is touch you and you respond." To prove his point, he touched her nipples with his thumbs. They hardened instantly. "See. That's so sexy. I love it. And I love the way your breath catches when I stroke them." Using his palms he made circles, lightly stroking the sensitive buds. Around and around, barely touching, until she reached her hands around to grasp his hips in order to push her chest forward, straining for more.

"Beau," she whispered, then gasped when his fingers replaced his palms.

"That's it. That's the little sound I love." He rubbed each rosy nipple between his thumb and index fingers then plucked at them. "So sexy. You like that, don't you?"

"Y-yes."

He palmed her breasts. "So soft and round." Then he squeezed ever so slightly. "Beautiful."

One hand continued its maddening attention to her breast while he skimmed his other hand down her rib cage, over her flat tummy to the tuft of soft brown hair between her thighs. He tested its softness, texture, slowly moving closer and closer to probe her feminine heat.

She moaned.

But when her eyelids drifted down, he'd have none of it. "No, don't stop watching. I want you to see how sexy you really are. How much I want you." And he slipped his finger between her soft folds, swollen with heat and need. "Oh, darlin'. You're so hot. Feel how hot you are." And while she watched, spellbound, he began to stroke her.

She whimpered and reached up her hands to clasp the back of his neck. "Beau...please..." She tried to close her eyes but she couldn't tear her gaze away from the reflection in the mirror. The reflection of a woman in the throes of passion, her body flushed with sweat and desire, her breath coming in short gasps as she squirmed and rotated her hips. She whimpered again, aching with need as he stroked her to the edge of madness.

"Please, oh please," she begged.

"That's it. Watch while you come for me. See your own pleasure. Yes. Oh, yes." She bucked, pumping her hips against his hand. Hard. Mercilessly. "So good." The first climax rolled through her, then another until her body shuddered with satisfaction and went limp. Then unable to stand not being inside her, he turned her in his arms, picked her up and carried her to the bed.

While he reached for a condom from the bedside table with one hand, the other continued to stroke the inside of her thighs, her soft, smooth belly and her breasts. He stopped only long enough to sheath himself with the condom and then parted her legs. Once more he stroked her, drove her almost to the edge, her entire slender body trembling with need. Then he entered her.

"*Yes.*" She dug her fingers into the hard flesh of his shoulder and planted feet flat on the bed, using them as leverage to thrust her body up. Hips undulating, pumping against his, she arched her back.

He moved slowly at first, thrusting in and out, driving deep then almost completely withdrawing, but not quite, in a torturous rhythm of pleasure that seemed to drive her mad, that she both hated and craved. She began to writhe, rolling her hips up to meet each powerful thrust and demand more. And more. Until finally she felt suspended in midair, waiting for the plunge into exquisite pleasure. Then her hold snapped and she plummeted, crying out.

As every muscle in his body strained to the point of breaking, he threw his head back and with a primitive groan he followed her into his own swirling release. And it went on and on, draining him, wringing him dry until there was nothing left but to settle back on solid ground.

The night was long—long enough for another journey to pleasure, then another, until finally they lay spent, snuggled together, and slept.

Hours later Beau slipped from the bed. Heading downstairs to make coffee, he turned at the door to look at her sleeping like a satisfied cat curled up on a pillow. He couldn't believe how they'd loved each other last night, each giving and taking with equal intensity. He'd never had that with any woman. She was special, he thought, closing the bedroom door. Very special.

Fifteen minutes later he slipped back into the room. "Hey. Wake up, sleepyhead."

Lily blinked, focusing on Beau standing beside the bed, two cups of coffee in his hands. "'Morning," she said, her voice hoarse. "What time is it?"

"Almost eleven. How about brunch?"

She stretched like a lazy cat. "Just coffee and toast."

"You want to shower first, or shall I?"

"Whatever." She yawned.

He rested one knee on the bed, leaned over and kissed her. "How about together?"

"Ah, water conservation."

He kissed her cheek, chin, earlobe then returned to nibble on her bottom lip. "Time conservation. We can get clean and sexy at the same time. And since you have to be home by one I want to make every minute count."

The shower lasted much longer than they planned and they never made it to brunch. All too soon Lily was in her car and Beau was standing by the window.

"I'll see you in three or four days." He leaned in the window and kissed her. "And get some rest while I'm gone."

THE MORNING AFTER BEAU left, Lily woke up feeling lousy. She attributed most of it to the fact that he was gone. No wonder they called this kind of feeling the blues, she thought. But as the day wore on she felt worse, bad enough, in fact, to go home early.

"It's no wonder you came down with something the way you've been working lately. If you're not better by the morning," Amelia said, serving Lily a bowl of potato soup in bed, "you need to call Dr. Morgan."

"I'm sure it's just the flu. Half the kids parading in and out of the library have got it. I'll be fine."

"Lily Catherine Matthews, this is your mother talking. Now, I want you to promise me you'll call the doctor if you're not feeling better tomorrow morning."

"I promise."

She would have promised anything, she thought, as her mother closed the bedroom door behind her, just for a little solitude. The flu was bad enough, but the blues made it ten times worse. She'd never felt so alone or lonely, yet company was the last thing she wanted. Except Beau's. Three more days before he returned, and she didn't even want to think about the nights. Flu or no flu she had to be well when he got back. Every minute with him was too precious. She had no intention of wasting them doctoring a stuffy nose or fever. So, she would keep her promise, see the family physician, Dr. Morgan, and be well in time to welcome Beau home.

7

"EXCUSE ME?" Lily stared at the elderly doctor seated behind his desk as if he'd just sprouted two heads. "Did you just say—"

"You heard me correctly. My tests indicate that you're pregnant."

"That's not possible," she said.

Dr. Morgan smiled. "I wish I had a nickel for every time I'd heard a woman say that to me. Were you taking birth control pills?"

"Yes, for about the last month or so and I used condoms for extra protection. That's why there must be some kind of mix-up in the lab results. I've heard of that happening."

"Did you use the condoms every time?"

"Yes, except...the first time."

"I don't mean to sound flippant, but once is all it takes. And as for the lab, there's no mistake. You are pregnant. I'd say three weeks along. When was your last period?" He flipped through her file. "Here it is. Yes, judging from the date of your last period and the fact that you've been one of those regular-as-clockwork types from the beginning, I'd say three weeks is a good guess." He closed the file and looked at her sitting across from him. "You had no idea, did you?"

Lily shook her head.

"But you must have realized you'd missed a period."

"I..." How could she tell him she'd been so enthralled with her torrid nights of passion that she hadn't even realized she'd missed a period? "I've been very busy with a new project."

"I'm sorry, my dear. I've known you since you were born and I can only imagine how this will affect you, to say nothing of your mother."

At the mention of her mother the shocked stupor she'd been in since she'd heard the word pregnant, evaporated. "She can't know."

"But, Lily—"

"No. You won't tell her, will you?"

"Of course not, but you can't keep this a secret unless..." He frowned for a second then pushed away from his desk and walked around to her. "Lily, I hope you don't mind if I speak as a longtime friend as well as your doctor."

"N-no...of...of course not."

"I'm sure you realize you have several options concerning your pregnancy."

"Options," she said, still trying to cope, trying to focus on his words.

"Do you think the baby's father will do right by you?"

It was such a totally old-fashioned term but it reminded Lily that Dr. Morgan knew her as well as anyone in her family, and cared about her. "My instinct is probably not, but I don't know for sure."

"Well, then maybe we should wait to review the rest of your options until—"

"No. Go ahead. I'd rather know everything."

"All right. You can keep your baby, of course, but considering...well, you know the obvious ramifications there. You can have the child and give it up, opting for either a sealed or open adoption." He thought for a moment, then said, "Arranging for you to be away from Rosemont might be tricky, but not impossible. And, lastly...you can terminate the pregnancy."

"No!" she said, instinctively.

"Lily, you don't have to make a decision now," he patted her shoulder, "and you shouldn't."

The gesture of comfort finally penetrated her haze of stunned disbelief and she started to cry. The chilling reality of the situation rushed over her like an Arctic tidal wave. Tears and more tears came as she recalled Beau's words the first time they'd been together.

The last thing I want is a little surprise wrapped in pink or blue.

"Thank...thank you, Dr. Morgan. No, I...I can't make a decision now."

"Don't worry, Lily. You've got time. And I'll help you in any way I can," he told her, offering another reassuring pat. "Why don't you take a few minutes to compose yourself before you walk back out into the reception area."

She took a deep breath, her tears slowly subsiding. "Yes."

"Have you had any morning sickness?"

Lily shook her head.

"That's good, but you might soon. I suggest keeping crackers by your bed to have if you wake up nauseous. I'll give you an antinauseau drug, just in case it gets bad, and some samples of vitamins to take because I don't think you should have a prescription filled in town. And I don't want you driving to Richmond today."

"Thanks."

"I need to see you again in a couple of weeks, but instead of calling the office for an appointment, tell my secretary that you have a book I asked you to locate." When she gave him a quizzical look, he added, "A white lie, but necessary I'm afraid. If you prefer, call it precaution against gossip." He handed her a small piece of paper along with the vitamin samples. "Here's my beeper number. Call me when you've made a decision, or if you just want to talk. In the meantime I want you to get plenty of sleep and try to eat good food."

Lily rose only to discover she was a little unsteady on her feet.

Dr. Morgan caught her elbow. "Okay? Would you like to lie down?"

"No. I'm fine. Really, Doctor."

"You need some time for the shock to wear off. Time to think about how you feel and what you want to do." He put an arm around her shoulder as he walked her to the door. "But while you're thinking, I want you to take good care of yourself, understand?"

"Yes."

"Good." He gave her shoulder a fatherly squeeze.

LILY MADE IT THROUGH the rest of the day on sheer determination not to fall apart. Now, the library just closed, she sat staring out her office window, still trying to wrap her mind around what had happened. Finally, with a soul-deep sigh, she closed her eyes and laid her head against the back of the chair.

She had no one but herself to blame for this pregnancy. No one. She'd let desire rule, instead of her head, and look where it had gotten her.

Dear Lord, pregnant!

The sheer stupidity and irresponsibility of what she'd done hung like a stone around her neck. What a fool she'd been! A self-centered, arrogant fool, thinking she could face the reality of pregnancy like a brave little soldier. What idiocy. She might indeed have to show a brave face to the rest of the world, but that didn't mean she could pretend to herself. She was scared spitless. Frantic. Terrified right down to her toes.

What was she going to do? How would she ever be able to cope...?

"Stop," she said. "Take a deep breath." She did, feeling a little less frenzied. Cope. That's what she had to do, and this sort of mindless panic wasn't helping. Her head actually ached from thinking about her situation. And nothing seemed any clearer now than when Dr. Morgan had given her the news of her situation. Her mind refused to be logical about...

Her situation?

Lily realized that maybe she couldn't sort out her problem because she hadn't seen it as it was. And the first step was to stop thinking of it as a "situation." She was pregnant. "It" was a...

"Baby," she whispered, the word sounding utterly foreign, yet comforting at the same time. "Baby."

Slowly she sat up straight in her chair. At last one thing was startlingly clear. With just one word she had eliminated at least one of her options. No matter what happened, she wouldn't, couldn't terminate this pregnancy. A new life was growing inside her, a life created out of passion and love, at least partly out of love, and she would do nothing to harm...her baby.

Gently she rested her hand over her still flat stomach. "My baby."

Hers *and* Beau's, her conscience reminded her.

But he didn't want any surprise bundles. And she couldn't blame him for feeling that way, given the circumstances of his own birth. She had to remember that Beau was a temporary spark in her life. The child she was carrying was not. Even if she decided to put the baby up for adoption it would always own a piece of her heart. For the rest of her life she would think about it, worry about it, wish...

Wish what? That she hadn't made a mistake? Wish that she'd kept her baby no matter what the cost?

The answer to both questions came to her as clear and sure as though a voice had boomed across the cosmos. And the answer was yes. She'd never been one to mull and stew over problems, but rather cut to the chase to find what was best, what was right. She might spend months putting her decisions into practice as she had with Beau, but the decision-making process had always been logical and straightforward. It was only the size of this problem that had made her feel so frantic, almost too frantic to take any course of action. Now, she realized that in her heart there had never been a decision to make. She could never give her child away any more than she could have an abortion. This baby was hers. She wanted it and she intended to keep it...no matter what.

One decision down and at least two more to go, Lily thought. First, if she told Beau about the baby, and it was a big *if*, how and when did she tell him? And second, how could she ever find the right words to tell her mother? Suddenly both questions loomed larger than her decision to keep her baby. Too large to deal with today. Procrastination went against her character, but she was too tired, too mentally wrung-out to continue. Besides, one life-changing decision a day was enough for anyone to be expected to handle. She had three days until Beau returned. Three days to decide her future and the future of her baby.

THREE DAYS LATER Lily had come to the conclusion that there was no reason Beau should have to pay for her mistake. Though how she'd been able to muddle through to a decision was still a mystery to her. Never in her life could she remember feeling so totally exhausted...or queasy. Fortunately for her, the morning sickness came almost as soon as she woke up. And, so far, she'd gotten by using the flu as an excuse, but that wouldn't hold up much longer. She still hadn't dealt with the issue of telling her mother, but Beau was her first priority. And since she was firm about him not knowing she was pregnant, there was only one way to make sure he never found out.

She had to end the relationship. Now. Today. Just as soon as he returned.

Easy enough to say, Lily thought as she went about her work in the solemn quiet of the library before the other employees began to arrive. But the realization that today would be the last day she would ever see Beau hit her hard. Never to feel his touch again, hear him call her "darlin'," was almost more than she could bear. But she had no choice. He'd never once mentioned love, never once given her any indication that he was interested in more than what they had. And what they had was purely physical. At least, as far as he was concerned. He had no idea she was in love with him, and now there was no reason for him ever to know. At this point, proclaiming her love would only be asking for more pain she didn't need.

So, she waited for his call. It came late in the afternoon.

"Hey, there, darlin'," he said as soon as she answered.

"Beau." She'd spent the past three days thinking about how she would act, what she would say the next time she spoke to him, but now her heart shot into her throat and she could hardly breathe. "How...how are you?"

"Better now that I hear your voice. I just called to

let you know I'll be back in Rosemont around four this afternoon."

"That's, uh, wonderful," she said, knowing nothing would truly be wonderful without him.

"Have dinner with me? I've got some news I want to share."

"All right."

"You sound funny. Are you okay?"

"No, not really. I've had the flu ever since you've been gone. In fact, now that I think about it, you might not want to be around me." Chicken, her conscience prodded.

"Darlin', if whatever you've got is contagious, I'd have already come down with it. I'll take my chances tonight. Say, around seven?"

"Seven is fine."

Lily hung up the phone and wanted to cry. She wanted to go home, lock herself in her room and cry until she couldn't cry another tear.

Cry until Beau was gone.

She wouldn't, of course. She had no choice but to play out the little scenario she'd dreamed up for Beau's benefit. She intended to tell him that she'd discovered that she wasn't as much of an adventuress as she'd originally thought. And the longer they were together the more she realized that their affair wasn't working. She would confess that after all was said and done, he'd known her better than she knew herself because, deep in her heart, she did want something more ordinary, more stable. And he'd been right. She wasn't the sneak-around-for-sex-on-the-sly type, after all. She'd convinced herself she could pull off the affair without any guilt, but it wasn't working. So, it was best that they simply go their separate ways. There was no one to blame. It just needed to end. No harm done.

Lily took a deep breath. She had to make her performance good, her reasoning plausible. Sad to say, but the rest of her life hinged on how well she could deceive the man she loved, the father of her child. No amount of justification would make that all right, but it was necessary.

BEAU WAS ALL SMILES when he opened the door. Until he got a good look at Lily.

"Darlin'." He took her hand and brought her inside. "Are you feeling worse?"

She shook her head. "I told you when I don't get enough sleep it shows on my face. Don't worry," she lied. "I don't feel as bad as I look. Just a little weak."

"You look beautiful like always. C'mon and sit down."

When he led her into the library Lily wanted to balk, to tell him, no, not here. Not in the place where they'd first made love. For one fleeting second she almost chickened out and told him she *did* feel bad after all. Bad enough that she had to go. But she hung on to her nerve. She sat down on the sofa and braced herself for what she had to do.

Beau sat beside her, kissed her forehead. "You poor baby. That flu bug really hit you hard, didn't it? Can I get you something?"

"I wish you'd stop fussing," she said, a slight edge in her voice. "I'm fine. Really."

He smiled. "That's my Lily." He put his arm around her and pulled her to him. "I've missed you."

Lily allowed herself the brief, sweet luxury of savoring his embrace. She put her hand on his chest, feeling the beat of his heart through her fingers. "I missed you, too." And would keep on missing him for a long time, she thought. Maybe forever.

"Well, being away from you was hard, but at least something good came out of it."

Lily sat up straight, knowing she needed distance. "Yes, how was your trip?"

"Great. Fantastic, in fact. I think I've settled the questions about the plant. I sold it," he announced. "I signed the papers this morning. It's a done deal and the employees will be notified the first of next week."

"But I thought you said that wasn't your first choice."

"It wasn't, but microchips aren't really my thing. I don't know much about that business and frankly,

I've got enough on my plate now. So, I cut the best deal possible."

"For whom?"

Beau looked at her, trying to figure out why the sudden chill in her voice. And unless it was his imagination she had actually scooted away from him. "For everybody. I made money and the plant stays open under a management that knows what it's doing. I sold the plant to TexTech, one of the biggest, most profitable companies in the country. Jobs are secure. In fact, the existing employees will all get a raise and they'll be hiring new people. I'd say that was a good deal, wouldn't you?"

"It certainly sounds like it."

"Not sounds like. Is." He frowned, studying her face. "I think I should take you home," he suddenly announced.

"Why?"

"Because I think you feel worse than you're telling me."

"I'm fine, I told you."

"Then what's wrong? And don't tell me nothing, because I know damned good and well that something is wrong." He put his finger under her chin, forcing her to look at him. "Tell me."

Her stomach was churning again and she was scared she might get sick. It was probably just nerves but she couldn't afford to take a chance. "I..." She put two fingertips to her temple. "I do have a slight headache. Could you get me a glass of water?"

"Sure." He walked over to the bar, reached for a glass and some ice.

While he filled the glass with water, Lily quickly reached inside her purse where she kept the bottle of prenatal vitamins and the antinausea pills Dr. Morgan had given her. She popped one of the pills into her mouth, but just as she was returning the bottle to her purse, Beau turned around and walked toward her. Hastily she tossed the bottle inside, then plopped her purse onto the floor beside the sofa. That had been a close call. If she wanted to pull this off, she had to be careful.

He handed her the glass of water. "Okay, let's have it," he said.

She got up and walked over to stand in front of the fireplace, keeping her back to him. If she had to look him in the eyes right now, she wasn't sure her courage would last. "I...I've done a lot of thinking since you've been gone, Beau."

"And?"

"And I think you were right in the beginning when you asked why I didn't find some nice local guy and get my adventure the old-fashioned way. I should have. I guess you knew me better than I knew myself, because now I realize I'm not cut out to be the sex-at-the-drop-of-a-hat kind of girl. I thought that's what I wanted, but it isn't. I'm sorry."

Beau couldn't believe what he was hearing. She couldn't be serious. *"Sorry,"* he said. "Is that all you've got to say?"

"What else can I say?"

"Try a decent explanation. Why are you doing an about-face all of a sudden?"

"Listen, I take full responsibility for this...situation. I came to you—"

"Damn right you did."

"And I'm the one who promised no strings, no regrets. Not that I have any regrets," she said, grasping at straws. "I...I'll always be glad that you were...well, you were wonderful. A great lover, but..."

"But you've changed your mind. Just like that."

"Yes. I don't know why you sound so shocked," she said. "It was just sex. That's all it was from the beginning. That's all you expected to give, all you expected from me. We made a bargain that worked for both of us...only it just doesn't for me anymore," she lied. "So, I think the best thing is for us to end it before there are regrets. Just walk away."

Just walk away!

Just sex!

Stunned, he couldn't believe she'd say that. In fact, how dare she say that. It wasn't just sex and it never had been. Well, maybe that first time, but after that it had become more. She was more to him than just a bargain. And she wasn't that good an actress to have been pretending all this time.

He didn't believe her.

Something else was going on here. She'd been too straightforward about everything to change her mind like this. He didn't know why, but he knew she was lying.

He took a step forward. "Dammit, Lily, I think there's more to this than what you're telling me—" As he stepped his foot tangled in her purse strap. Frustrated, he kicked the purse off his shoe. It rolled, spilling some of the contents. "I'm not going to stand here—" he bent down and picked up a bottle, intending to put it back in her purse "—and let you ruin it with some unreasonable—"

The label on the bottle stopped him dead in his tracks.

Prenatal? Prenatal. Didn't that mean... He looked up. Her back was still to him.

"What are these for?"

"What?" Lily turned to face him and almost fainted. She swallowed hard, fighting tears and panic.

"These." He held up the bottle.

"I...I—don't know what you're talking about?"

"Why do you have prenatal vitamins?"

"Oh, those." She dismissed the importance of his question with a wave of her hand and hoped he didn't notice it was shaking. "They're just sort of heavy-duty vitamins. The doctor thought I needed some extra stuff to help kick this flu bug, and since those are—"

"For pregnant women."

She shrugged nonchalantly. "Anyone can take them."

Beau looked at her, his mind fitting together the events of the past week like pieces of a jigsaw puzzle. Lily looking tired and like she'd lost weight. The onset of the flu, or what looked like flu. Her reserve when she first arrived. Out of the blue, her decision to break off their relationship. And now prenatal vitamins. Coincidence? He didn't think so. His logical little librarian, his straightforward, get all her ducks in a row Lily was lying through her teeth.

"I don't believe you," he said flat out. "They're yours."

"I just said I was taking them, but not the way you think. I—"

"You're pregnant, aren't you?"

"That's...that's ridiculous."

"Is it?"

"Absolutely. Whatever put such an insane idea in your—"

"These damn vitamins for a start."

"I told you—"

"It doesn't hold water. Now, tell me the truth. Are you pregnant? Is that why this sudden change of heart? This 'it just doesn't work anymore' crap."

"I don't see why you're getting so angry."

"Angry! You think this is angry? You've never seen me angry. But you're about to if you don't stop trying to squirm out of telling me the truth. And so help me God, if this is some elaborate ploy—"

"Ploy? Oh, now I see why you've gotten on your high horse. This is about your ego. I'm the one walking away and you can't stand it. The devastating Beau Stuart just might not be so irresistible after all. Wounded ego. That's all this is." Desperate people did desperate and unreasonable things. Suddenly Lily found herself babbling and unable to stop. Through some twisted level of reasoning, the longer she talked, the safer she felt.

Beau stared at her. She was ranting. His logical Lily was ranting.

"You've got to have some logical reason why I'm leaving instead of drooling all over you and you'll jump at any excuse, even one this absurd."

Now he knew she was pregnant. And he was beginning to understand why she was deliberately turning her back on him.

"You know, I never wanted to believe all the stories about your colossal ego, but now I see it was all true. As long as you're getting what you want on your terms everything is hunky dory, but let someone stand up and exercise her rights, forget it. And I'm not hanging around for more of your maniacal raving. I'm leaving." She stomped off toward the door.

"Stop right where you are."

"I'm through being insulted—"

"You're not leaving this room until you answer my question."

"The hell I will."

"The hell you won't." He grabbed her by the arm. "Now, dammit to hell, are you pregnant?"

"Let go of me."

"Answer me."

"No." She jerked her arm free.

"Answer me," he roared. "Are...you...pregnant?"

"Yes," she roared right back.

There was only a slight pause before he answered.

"Then we're getting married."

8

LILY OPENED HER MOUTH to speak, then closed it again. Her heart was hammering so loudly in her ears they hurt. "You're crazy."

"Maybe." No maybe about it. He was as shocked at his proposal as she was, but he'd made the offer and he'd never reneged on a deal in his life.

"Marriage isn't the answer. I never intended to tell you about the baby."

"I figured as much."

"Well, I'm sorry I didn't stick by my original decision. You don't want to get married. You told me so yourself that first night. And you're not in love with me, are you?" She waited for some response, and couldn't keep from hoping. "No, of course not. And I'm not in love with you." A white lie, but she had to protect herself.

"How the hell should I know?" he snapped. "I've never been in love. But it doesn't make any difference. You're pregnant and I'm the father. Whether you did this deliberately or not, I know it's mine, and I don't walk away from my responsibilities."

His words cut her as surely as if he'd taken a knife

to her heart. Not only did he not love her, but he actually thought she was capable of scheming to trap him. "I'm not your responsibility and neither is my baby."

"Our baby. And just out of curiosity, how did this 'accident' happen? You told me you were protected."

"I was...or at least I thought I was. I told you I'd only been taking birth control pills for a short time. That's why I wanted you to use a condom. To be double sure this didn't happen."

"Then when—"

"That first night. We...I didn't really know how fast...I never expected... It doesn't matter. I let things get out of hand and I am the one responsible."

"It takes two to tango," he said, furious with her and himself for allowing this to happen. "I took your word and didn't bother to take my own precautions. So, whether you planned this or not, doesn't make any difference."

The hurt was fading and in its place came anger. "It makes a difference to me. You think I deliberately got myself pregnant? That I purposely set out to concoct a wild scheme with you as the prize? Is your ego so huge that you think I'd risk being a social outcast and risk my mother's mental health just to snag the great Beau Stuart?" She shook her head. "You're not crazy. You're just a garden variety ass."

"Well, from now on you're stuck with an ass because no child of mine is going to grow up the way I did. We're getting married and that's all there is to it."

"No," she insisted vehemently.

"Yes," he calmly replied.

They stared at each other, poised like two boxers waiting for the bell to signal the next round in their match.

Finally Lily regained enough self-control to realize this would only end in both of them saying things they would regret. She needed to stay calm to make him understand that what he was suggesting would never work.

She took a deep breath, releasing it slowly. "This isn't getting us anywhere." And she walked back to the sofa and plopped down.

"On that we both agree."

"Listen to me. I really do appreciate your spur-of-the-moment offer, but—"

"Now, hold on—"

"No. Let me finish, please. This whole thing was my idea. I came to you. I'm the one who wanted no strings and you were in complete agreement. Why don't we just leave it at that? I don't want anything from you, Beau. I'll even sign a document saying neither I, nor the baby, have any claim on you or your money. Just have your lawyer draw up something and I'll sign it. At the same time he can draw up a paper that relieves you of all parental rights. You sign your paper, I sign mine, and we go our separate ways. It's as simple as that."

Beau personally knew at least ten guys that had been in similar situations who would have killed for the kind of deal she was offering. He'd be a fool not to take her up on it. An idiot, in fact. It was what he wanted, wasn't it? To walk away scot-free. Then it occurred to him she might be thinking of an abortion. It didn't figure, not with her background, but it was possible. The thought made him break out in a cold sweat.

"If I...we, do that, what will you do about the baby?"

"I'm having it."

"What about your mother?"

Briefly Lily closed her eyes. He'd hit the one mammoth hurdle in all of her reasoning and planning. "I don't know exactly how I'll handle that part of it. Maybe by taking a job in another town. I don't know yet, but I'll find a way. This child is going to be born, and loved and cared for. That's the only thing I know for sure at the moment." Then, as if that bit of determined assurance had drained the last of her energy, she sighed and laid her head on the back of the sofa.

Beau walked to the bar, poured himself a drink and downed half of it. There were so many emotions swirling around in him he was torn between wanting to shake her until her teeth rattled, and wanting to take her in his arms to comfort her. God, what a situation! His initial reaction had been to walk out without a backward glance. Instead he'd asked, no insisted, that she marry him. He was still in shock over that one. But he meant what he'd said. No child of his was growing up feeling like an outsider.

Outsider. That's what Lily would be if she stayed in this town and braved the gossip. Even if she moved to another city she would be alone, just her and the child. He killed the rest of his drink and reached for the bottle again. Of course, there was the possibility that she might...

Beau stopped, his hand in midreach. Might what, meet someone? Marry someone else? Allow someone else to raise his baby?

Less than a week ago, standing in the New Orleans airport, he'd been blindsided by the realization that he wanted just her. But that had been a mild jolt compared to the right-between-the-eyes blow at the thought of Lily with another man. Kissing him, touching him, making... No. She was his. She belonged to him. He loved...

He loved her.

Such a simple thing, he thought, truly startled at how simple it was. And how good it felt. He loved Lily. He loved her and she was having his baby. Suddenly he felt almost giddy. Bursting with emotion he turned to her...and discovered she was asleep.

He walked back to the sofa and stared down at her. What a fool he'd been. She was right. He'd been acting like an ass. But it wasn't every day a man found out he was going to be a father and a husband in the same day. Funny, he thought. His first reaction had been to propose. Now he understood why. He must have been in love with her for days, maybe even from the beginning, and didn't fully realize it until tonight. Then he remembered something Lily had said earlier.

You're not in love with me, are you? No, of course not. And I'm not in love with you.

He wouldn't accept that. She had to care. A woman didn't melt at the slightest touch the way she did unless she had some feeling for the man doing the touching. A woman didn't give herself completely, body *and* soul without at least a spark of love in her heart. Not a woman like Lily. No matter how it started, somewhere along they way they had both fallen in love. He'd bet his life on it. Who was he kidding? He *was* betting his life on it. Now all he had to do was make her believe he loved her and she loved him.

The simplest, most direct approach was to tell her he loved her, but he knew that wasn't going to work. Not now. Not after he'd practically accused her of lying and scheming. Beau winced, remembering how he'd spoken to her. No woman in her right mind would tumble into the arms of a man that insensitive. Besides, if anyone knew how determined Lily could be when she made up her mind, he did. She was dead set on taking total responsibility for this child and pushing him out of her life.

"No way, darlin'," he whispered. "No way I'm going to lose you now."

He needed a plan. Exactly what kind of plan he wasn't sure. But one thing he did know—she might be hardheaded, but he was no slouch in the determination department himself. For tonight he would let her think she'd won. Besides, she looked as if a good stiff breeze would blow her on her fanny. The dark circles beneath her eyes worried him. Starting tomorrow, things were going to change, beginning with her taking better care of herself.

Resisting the urge to scoop her into his arms, carry her up to his bed and tuck her in, Beau settled for gently touching her cheek. "Lily."

"W-what?" she asked, coming awake. "Oh." She sat up. "I didn't realize...we were talking. I apologize—"

"Don't worry about it. Looks like you've won for tonight anyway. Let me take you home."

"I have my car."

"Are you awake enough to drive?" He offered her a hand up.

She ignored it and stood by herself. "I'll be fine."

"Stubborn to the end, huh? All right," he said, following her out of the library to the front door.

Lily opened the door then turned back. "I'm sorry it has to end like this, Beau, but I'm sure by tomorrow you'll be glad. You'll go back to your life and this will all fade to a memory. You'll see."

"You think so?"

"Yes. And for what it's worth, I hope your memories will be pleasant. Mine will be." With that she turned and hurried out the door, got into her car and drove off.

It was all Beau could do not to run after her, but he knew it wouldn't do any good. She had to be persuaded to accept his love and trust her own. He smiled. A tough campaign lay ahead, but he was more than man enough for the job.

LILY DRAGGED HERSELF out of bed, into the shower and dressed for work, the memory of last night clinging to her like the aftereffects of a mind-numbing drug. She went into breakfast dreading the day. A day without Beau.

Amelia had just dropped bread into the toaster when Lily walked into the kitchen. "Good morning, dear."

"Morning." She reached over to the credenza on the other side of the table and turned on the radio for the local news and weather. The announcer's voice filled the room.

"News at the top of the hour. Stuart Electronics, Rosemont's largest employer, has been sold to TexTech Industries. Beau Stuart, former owner of the microchip plant,

has called a press conference at noon today at city hall to provide details of the sale. On the statewide scene..."

When Lily saw the worried look on her mother's face, she snapped off the radio. "It's nothing to be concerned about, Mom. I talked—" The ringing of the doorbell cut her off. "I'll get it." She left the room and came back a moment later, carrying a note.

"Who was that, dear?"

"A delivery."

"Delivery? From whom?"

Lily looked up from staring at the envelope in her hand. "Beau Stuart."

Amelia stopped buttering the toast that had just popped out of the toaster. "Why would he be sending a letter by special delivery?"

The note was addressed to Lily Matthews and Amelia Jackson Matthews. She was almost afraid to open it. Once before, she had entertained the idea that he might divulge her secret, and Lord knew he had a lot more ammunition now. And he'd been angry last night. Angry enough for revenge? Despite everything that had happened, she still couldn't see Beau being deliberately cruel.

"Well, aren't you going to open it?" Amelia asked.

"It's addressed to both of us."

"It's all right. Go ahead."

Lily opened the envelope, took out the folded piece of paper and read. "He's sending a car for us to drive us to the press conference today."

"Well, that's very nice, but—"

"He says he'll also address the restoration project and that since it pertains to our family he'd like for us to be present."

"Oh, of course. That makes sense."

"But I thought..."

"Thought what, dear?"

"I didn't think he was ready to go public with the project yet, or that he even wanted people to know his part in it."

"Maybe he changed his mind, or maybe the mayor is making an announcement."

"Maybe," Lily said, still not sure what had prompted the change.

"But I don't think I can go. I haven't been any-where but the grocery store in so long I wouldn't know how to act."

Lily knew her mother was trying to make light of the situation, but she also knew the idea of appearing in public terrified her.

"You go along, dear, and represent both of us. Maybe you could ask Aunt Pauline—"

"I'm not going without you," Lily announced.

"But, Lily—"

"No. You're the last surviving member of Tobias Jackson's family and you have to go." All of which was true, but what she didn't say was that she didn't want to face Beau alone.

"I know you mean well, Lily, but I can't. You understand."

"Mother—"

At that moment Pauline swept through the back door without knocking, waving an envelope in her hand identical to the one that had just been delivered to Lily and her mother.

"You won't believe the colossal nerve of that Beau Stuart," Pauline said, then stopped short when she saw the envelope in Lily's hand. "Oh, I see you got one, too." She glanced at Amelia. "You're not going."

"Of course not, how could I? But Lily insists she won't go without me."

"Impossible," Pauline huffed.

"Aunt Pauline, I know you mean well, but—"

"I'm only looking out for you and your mother. I understand you have to make an appearance, Lily. After all, some people are already aware of your involvement with the project. Goodness knows that's generated enough talk. If you don't show up it will only add to the gossip."

"Gossip," Amelia said, disheartened. "Sometimes I think this town would shrivel up and die if the gossip ceased."

"Don't upset yourself, Amelia. I'm certain Lily will handle the situation with grace and charm. After all, she has Matthews blood in her veins."

Her mother wasn't ready to face a public appearance and Lily was beginning to think she never would. Chances of that ever happening would disappear for sure if she had to deal with being the grandmother of an illegitimate child. Lily's heart ached and she felt torn between wanting to protect her mother and wanting to make sure her child never had to live the way she had—in constant fear of causing more talk. "All right," Lily agreed.

THERE WAS A LARGER CROWD for the press conference than Lily expected, but she figured most were there out of curiosity. More fuel for the gossip mill, she thought, standing at the foot of the steps leading into city hall. A few feet away a small podium had been set up with microphones. Nearby Beau and Mayor Caldwell had their heads together in a last-minute conference. When Beau saw her coming up the steps he'd smiled tenderly, and she thought she could actually feel her heart breaking. Why did life have to be so hard sometimes?

"Ah, Lily, There you are," Caldwell said, coming to greet her.

"Hello, Lily," Beau said. "Nice to see you again."

At least she didn't have to worry about him not keeping up the facade. "Hello, Beau. Good to have you back in town."

"Well, it's noon on the dot," Caldwell said. "Let's get started, shall we?"

Lily and Beau followed him to the podium and

stood quietly while the mayor made a statement about city pride and progress, then surprisingly he turned the whole thing over to Beau.

"Thank you," Beau said, after a smattering of applause following his introduction. "I'm here today to put your minds to rest concerning the sale of Stuart Electronics. As reported, the sale is final, but it does not mean the plant is closing. In fact, the new owner, TexTech is anxious to increase production and increase personnel. So, not only will all present employees keep their jobs, but new jobs will be created."

That brought a round of genuine and robust applause so long that Beau finally had to hold up his hands to continue.

"And now that I've relieved a few minds, I'd like to tell you about a project I hope will also benefit the community and all of its citizens. I have recently donated the Stuart mansion as a historical museum in the hope that the house and its contents will be preserved as part of our national heritage. The house was built by Tobias Jackson in 1856 and will be restored to its original condition. I've created and funded a foundation to oversee the restoration and I'm pleased to announce that managership of that foundation is awarded to a prominent Rosemont citizen, and a member of the Jackson family, Rosemont's head librarian, Miss Lily Matthews."

Lily was stunned. She had had no idea he would

go this far. If she hadn't been standing on the steps to city hall in front of all these people she would have run like the devil. Instead she smiled while the crowd applauded. But it was all she could do to maintain her smile a second later when Beau stepped back, took her hand and pulled her up to the podium.

"I'm sure you'll all join me in congratulating Miss Matthews and know that your history is in the best possible hands."

Lily knew her cheeks were red and the people probably thought it was due to embarrassment. Little did they know it was more from anger. She couldn't wait to get off these steps and give Beau a piece of her mind.

"And now to celebrate all of this good fortune," he continued, "I'm inviting the entire population of Rosemont to a party. Mayor Caldwell has graciously consented to grant a permit for an event, so this Friday night there will be a party right here in the town square. Food, live music, amusements and rides for the kids and you're all my invited guests. Thank you, and see you Friday night."

As the applause rolled up from the audience, Beau stepped back, his hand still on Lily's arm, and led her away while the mayor took over.

"I can't believe you did that without telling me," she said once they were out of earshot of the crowd. "You had no right to make a public announcement without my permission. I'm going to wash my hands of the whole thing."

"No, you're not."

"I most certainly am. I have no intention of working with a liar. You told me you didn't want any public recognition. What do you call this press conference?"

"I changed my mind."

"Oh, just like that. You've changed your mind and that makes it okay?"

"Look who's talking."

She had no comeback for that. "What do you think you're doing?" she said as he hurried her toward his car.

"Taking you home."

"No, thanks. I'll walk."

He stopped, smiled and nodded to several people as they passed by. "Really," he said in a voice just loud enough for anyone close to hear. "I understand that's very good exercise for women who—"

"No!"

"—need it," he finished, took her arm and started walking again. "Of course, that doesn't include you."

"You did that on purpose," she said. "You deliberately scared me."

"Had to get your attention some way." He helped her into the car, closed her door, then went around and got in. "Now, if you'll calm down we'll have a reasonable conversation."

"You call threatening me reasonable?"

"You call making decisions concerning the future of my child without considering me fair?"

"Beau, we went over all this last night and you agreed."

"No. I just stopped arguing and let you think you have the last word."

"But—"

"No buts. Or ifs, or ands. I told you. No child of mine is going to grow up the way I did. He's going to have a name and a father."

"Beau, don't do this. You're only making matters worse."

"That's your department."

"What are you talking about?"

"All you have to do is marry me and everything is taken care of. The baby will have a name and you won't have a scandal."

"It won't work. I gave you all the reasons it won't work last night and nothing has changed."

She had no idea how much had changed. After she left last night it hadn't taken him long to realize the only plan he needed was persistence. He would continue to ask her to marry him. Knowing her stubborn streak she would probably continue to say no. That was okay. He had time and patience. He would wear her down. And when her resistance was at its ebb he would tell her how much he loved her, how much he wanted her and the baby. And she would believe him because she would see it in his eyes, hear it in his voice and know that it was true.

And his persistence plan had developed an unexpected byproduct. Somewhere along the way he'd realized he no longer held any animosity toward the people of Rosemont. His love for Lily had given him that freedom and he wanted and intended to make it part of their life together.

"Did you hear me?" she demanded.

"Oh, I heard you. I just don't accept your answer."

"Why not?"

"Because I think you need me."

She folded her arms across her chest and looked straight ahead. "You're wrong."

"Doubt it."

"You're making me mad, Beau."

"I can live with that."

"Well, live with this. I don't want you around. You were fine for sex, but now I'm through with you. There, satisfied? You've made me say things I didn't want to say. You and I are over."

"What if I said that I loved you?"

Her head snapped around and she looked at him, then quickly looked away. "I—I...I wouldn't believe you."

"That's what I figured." He started the car. *But you*

wanted to, he thought. That moment when she'd looked into his eyes searching for the truth had given him the hope he needed. She could protest all she wanted to and nothing would stop him from pursuing her.

"What is that cryptic response supposed to mean?"

"You figure it out, darlin'."

But she couldn't figure it, or him, out. She'd given him his freedom and he hadn't taken it. Why? Before she could come up with a logical answer he pulled the car up in front of her house and killed the engine. He helped her out of the car. Expecting him to drive away she was shocked to see him following her.

"What do you think you're doing?"

"Well, your mother and aunt missed the ceremony, so..." He shrugged. "If the mountain won't come to Mohammed..." He opened the door.

"Beau, you wouldn't...you promised—"

His grin was positively devilish as he ushered her past him and into the house. For her ears only he said, "All bets are off, darlin'."

Amelia and Pauline looked up as Beau and Lily came through the door, both women clearly stunned.

"Mom, you remember Beau Stuart."

"Y-yes."

"Beau, this is my aunt, Pauline Jackson. Aunt Pauline, Beau Stuart."

"Well, I am surely glad to finally meet you, Mrs. Jackson. Lily brags about you all the time."

Pauline offered a weak handshake. "You don't say."

"Oh, yes, ma'am, I do. She goes on and on about how she gets her love of history from you. That's why I was so sorry you two ladies couldn't make the press conference today. Especially since I know you must be proud of the fact that Lily will be in complete charge of the Stuart House foundation and museum. With a suitable compensation for her efforts, of course."

Lily looked at him. "Compensation? You never mentioned anything about money."

"Didn't I?" Beau rocked back and forth on his heels in a blatantly self-satisfied gesture. "Guess it slipped my mind."

Lily didn't know whether crying or screaming would bring her the greatest pleasure at that moment. He'd set it up so she would have an income. He was taking care of her despite the fact that she'd told him she didn't want or need his help. Suddenly she had the answer to her earlier question of why. He wanted some kind of hold on the baby. That's what it had to be. He might not want to be a father now, but he was hedging his bets against the future. "I don't want your money," she blurted.

"Lily," her mother said. "That sounded so rude."

"What I meant was, uh, that I love working on the house and it's connected to our family, so I feel uncomfortable taking money."

"But you should," Pauline interjected. "It's hard work, long hours and there's nothing wrong with being paid for your time."

"Mrs. Jackson," Beau said. "I couldn't have put it better myself. You are a very astute, sensible woman. Admirable qualities, I might add." He turned to Lily, actually shaking his finger at her and said, "You should listen to your aunt," then turned back to Pauline. "Thank you for pointing out the sensible thing to do."

"You're...you're welcome." Pauline frowned, obviously not sure how she wound up agreeing with Beau.

Now Lily knew what would make her feel better. A scream. And maybe a couple of stomps of her foot thrown in for good measure. The man was insufferably arrogant, pushy and egotistical—everything everybody said about him. She couldn't get him out of her house fast enough. "Thank you for seeing me home, Beau. Please don't let us keep you—"

"Oh, you're not keeping me from anything. And, to be honest, I had an ulterior motive in escorting you. I had hoped to be able to enlist your help," again he turned to Pauline, "Mrs. Jackson. And, of course, Mrs. Matthews."

"Me...mine?" Pauline sputtered.

"Certainly. This project is getting bigger by the day and I don't want just anyone working on it. I want the best. I wouldn't dream of looking anywhere else for Lily's assistants. After all, you three are the Jackson family."

"You want us to help Lily?" Pauline asked.

"Yes, ma'am. I'm sure you know that people around here haven't exactly gone out of their way to be friendly and that they've talked about me over back fences—not that either of you ladies fall into that category. You both have too much class for that. That's another reason I hope you consent to help Lily. Your names connected to the project would sure be a plus." Beau ducked his head then looked up at the two older women and smiled. "Hope I haven't insulted you."

Lily had been silent until now, mostly because she'd been fascinated watching him work on her aunt. But now she felt she had to step in. "Very nice, but—"

"Well, young man," Pauline said, "I'll give you this. You've got guts. And brains. You're right about our endorsement."

"Does that mean—"

Pauline held up her hand. "Hold on. I didn't say yes. Not sure I'm going to, and I certainly can't speak for Amelia."

"Mrs. Jackson, I'm just thrilled that you would even *consider* lending your assistance. I wonder...I hope you don't think I'm overstepping any boundaries here, but I wonder if you and Mrs. Matthews, and Lily, of course, would do me the honor of joining me for dinner? To celebrate Lily's appointment as head of the foundation."

Lily thought she might throw up, but not from morning sickness. He was so syrupy, so sticky sweet, a child could see through what he was doing. She expected her aunt to send him packing.

"Dinner?"

"I understand the Williamsburg Room at the Rosemont hotel has excellent food," Beau said, naming the most expensive and prestigious dining spot in town.

"Oh, my, the Williamsburg Room. Well, I... What do you think, Amelia?"

Lily couldn't believe her ears. Was her aunt actually considering accepting his offer?

"I think that's a very generous offer," Amelia said.

Beau grinned. "Not at all, Mrs. Matthews. No man in his right mind would miss the chance to enjoy the company of three—" he looked at Lily "—beautiful—" he looked at Pauline "—intelligent, and—" he looked at Amelia "—courageous women. I hope you all say yes."

Lily started to answer, declining for all of them when she looked at her mother and aunt. The two women were staring at Beau as if they were mesmerized. They'd actually bought into that butter-wouldn't-melt-in-his-mouth charm, she realized with shock.

"Well," Beau said, still smiling. "I guess I'd better be going."

"Oh, of course." Pauline came out of her haze.

"Lily, walk Mr. Stuart to the door," her mother said.

A moment later Lily stepped outside with Beau leading the way to his car. She had something to say to him and she didn't want the others to hear.

"Do you know what you've just done?"

"I've got a rough idea. I've gone public all the way."

"Exactly. You broke your promise."

"I promised not to make our, shall we say, clandestine meetings public, and I intend to keep that promise. What I'm doing now has nothing to do with that."

"Oh, I have never seen or heard so much bull as I just witnessed. You're proud of yourself, aren't you? You turned on the flattery and made two conquests. Brother, have you got them fooled. They think you're so charming. Personally," she added, thoroughly annoyed with him and her relatives, "I don't see it anymore."

"Look closer." He pulled her into his arms and there, in full view of whoever cared to look, kissed her. There was nothing charming about the kiss. It was hard, deep, devastating...and all too brief.

"That should hold you until tonight. Be ready at seven."

9

WHEN LILY ARRIVED at the library the following morning there was an arrangement of no less than three dozen roses on her desk. She pulled a single long stem from the bouquet and inhaled its fragrance. Even before she opened the card she knew who'd sent them. The card read:

I don't give up easy.
Beau.

That was what worried her. His determination rivaled her own. When she had called him last night to cancel dinner, he'd promptly responded with an invitation for his "three favorite ladies" to be his special guests at the party on the square Friday night. And when she told him she doubted her mother would ever agree, he'd simply said, "We'll see."

The man was as relentless as a pit bull. An attribute she was sure he found useful in business, but from her point of view, it was dangerous. If he'd made up his mind to stay connected to the baby, she had a war on her hands, and she knew it. And she was outgunned. Beau had enough money to hire an army of bulldog lawyers while she didn't even know how she was going to make a life for her and her child. Well, let him bring in his heavy artillery, she thought. She wasn't going to roll over and play dead for him. And she wasn't going to marry him.

There was a knock on her door and, before she could answer it, Beau strolled in. He smiled, seeing her with the rose to her nose. "Glad you like the flowers."

Lily quickly discarded the rose, "Wildly extravagant, if you ask me."

"That's what money is for."

"When you have a great deal."

"Marry me and you'll be rich."

"No." She leaned against the front edge of her desk and crossed her arms. "But that reminds me," she said, ignoring his proposal. "I'm not sure I can accept the 'compensation' you talked about yesterday. I told you that I didn't want anything from you."

He grinned. "Get over it."

"Why are you doing this?" she asked, hoping against hope she could make him understand he had to give up. Marriage was out of the question. It would be hard enough to raise a child alone. She wasn't going to make matters worse by marrying a man who didn't love her.

"I thought I made that very clear."

"Marriage."

"Exactly." He walked up to her, less than a foot of distance between them. "Did I mention how beautiful you look this morning? Those dark circles are disappearing. Must mean you're sleeping better. Glad one of us is. You were only in my bed one night but it sure seems empty now," he told her, his voice low, husky.

"I—I…" She'd been prepared for a full-out assault, not this seductive approach. Lily knew how susceptible she was to his sex appeal and knew she was on thin ice. She cleared her throat. "I slept just fine, thank you."

"Good, then you'll be able to work tonight."

"No," she told him.

"Why not?"

"I should think the answer to that question would be obvious."

"Oh, you mean because we used the project as an excuse so we could—"

"Yes." She didn't want him to finish. Her imagination didn't need any help with reminders of their time together. All of that wild, hot sex. All of that great, wild, hot sex.

"Well, that doesn't change the fact that the work still has to be done, and you are the manager of the foundation. Or are you going to walk away from the project, too."

"Of course not."

"Then I'll expect you tonight?"

Trapped. She was damned if she did and damned if she didn't. "Yes, but..."

"But what?"

"I think we should consider moving our base of operations from your house. Possibly find a small storefront office where we'd be more visible. Maybe it would get us some volunteers." No way was she going to tell him the real reason was that she didn't want to be alone with him. In his house. So close to his bedroom.

"I'll think about it. In the meantime, my house around six-thirty? I'll send out for dinner."

"Fine," she said. "Only don't order for me."

"You have to eat."

"Oh, I'll eat. Just not with you." Feeling secure in having the last word, she walked to her office door and opened it. "Thanks again for the flowers and for stopping by."

Beau grinned, strolled to the door and gave her a quick kiss on the cheek. "Tonight." Then he was gone.

Damned if he didn't get the last word, she thought, annoyed. Tonight. A statement, not a question. More important, was it a threat or a promise?

That question nagged Lily all day. As she drove to the Stuart mansion she renewed her promise to herself not to give in to her weakness for Beau. But when he opened the door he looked so handsome, so incredibly sexy in jeans and a silk shirt, sleeves rolled to midforearm, she felt her resolve sag.

"C'mon in."

Said the spider to the fly, she thought. Strength was the word for the day. *Be strong, Lily. Be strong.*

Beau showed her into the library, then went to the bar and brought back a soft drink and handed it to her. "No wine for you. Not good for the baby."

"I knew that."

"By the way, how are you feeling? And before you dismiss me with the noncommittal 'fine,' be prepared. If you don't keep me posted on your health, I'll talk to your doctor."

"You wouldn't."

"Wouldn't I? I'm the father, remember."

"My health and the health of *my* baby is privileged information."

Beau's temper flared, but the only outward sign was the flash of his eyes. "Don't push me, Lily. Now, I'll ask again. How are you feeling?"

She recognized the edge in his voice and decided not to antagonize him further. "I...I've had some morning sickness." She begrudged him even that much information because it felt like giving him little pieces of herself and he had enough of her already. But she knew if she didn't cooperate he would just bulldoze over her, albeit with charm, just as he'd done with her mother and aunt. He was good at it.

Expert, in fact. And if she was being honest with herself, his charm was an effective weapon against her.

"Bad?"

She shook her head, relenting. "The doctor gave me some pills. Mostly I'm just tired all the time."

"Why didn't you say so before." He took her soft drink and led her to the sofa. "Here." He pulled her down beside him then turned her sideways so her back was to him, and began massaging her shoulders. "Relax. You're way too tense."

She had to admit it felt good. He worked over her shoulders and neck, his fingers pressing, massaging. Gradually she began to relax, her body becoming pliant beneath his touch. Eventually, the massage began to feel good in ways that had nothing to do with relaxation. She could feel his breath through the thin cotton of her shirt, on the back of her neck. Her whole body tingled.

"Feels good, doesn't it?"

She nodded, not trusting her voice.

"You could stand to have this done every day. It's great for the baby, too."

She sighed. Knowing she shouldn't, yet unable to stop, she gave herself over to the pleasure of his hands on her body.

"And you're sleeping okay?"

She nodded.

"And eating right?"

Another nod, plus a "hmm."

"Good." His hands worked down her arms to her fingers. "Any aches, pains?"

"No," she whispered. "Just some..."

He massaged his way back up her arms to her neck. "Some what?"

"T-tenderness."

"Where?" His hands skimmed over her collarbone to the swell of her breasts. "Here?"

Some rational part of her brain tried desperately to remind her she was treading on dangerous ground, but she tuned it out. "Y-yes."

Gently he massaged her flesh through her shirt. "Does that hurt?"

She could only shake her head. The combined sensations of pleasure and pain was so sweet she wanted to cry out for him never to stop.

"More?"

"Yes," she said on a low moan as he cupped her.

"So soft." His thumbs stroked her nipples through the cotton fabric and he felt them harden instantly. "Soft, sweet."

She whimpered, arching her back and it was all the invitation he needed. He unbuttoned the top button of her shirt, the second...

Lily's eyes flew open. "No," she whispered, her hands pushing his away. She was a button away from begging him to make love to her. "No." She stood up, quickly putting herself back together.

"Did I do something wrong? I didn't massage too hard, did I?"

She couldn't believe it. He actually had the nerve to look as if he didn't have a clue why she'd put a stop to his little game. Anger flashed through her, partly directed at him, partly at herself for allowing him to get under her skin and very nearly under her clothes. She wanted to slap his face.

"If I were a man I'd deck you."

"Then it's a good thing for me you're not." He stood up so close to her she had to step back. "And a good thing for you, considering how much of a woman you are, if I remember correctly."

She hated the way he got to her with just a few well-chosen and usually suggestive words. Mainly because she had very little defense against it. Her own vivid memories of their lovemaking didn't help.

Lovemaking?

They'd never made love because it was only sex as far as he was concerned. She had to hang on to that, Lily reminded herself. It just might be her salvation. She picked up her purse and turned to leave.

"Where are you going?"

"Home."

"Lily." He reached for her, but she backed away.

"I don't want you to touch me."

"The hell you don't. A moment ago—"

"A moment ago I forgot how ruthless you can be."

"Only when I want something " he said, the heat of his gaze scorching as it drifted over her.

"I know." She clutched her purse to her chest like a shield. "That's the problem."

"Marry me," he said softly.

"N-no." And she was out the door before he could catch up to her.

A few seconds later Beau stood watching her tail-lights disappear down the driveway. "Close, but no cigar," he said to the night.

But he could live with that because he'd proved she would still respond to him. Respond quick and hot. Her need was every bit as great as his. And despite how much willpower she possessed, he had a secret weapon. Love. He would use all his love, all his desire, to break down her resistance. And he was positive in the end she would willingly open the door to her heart.

Time to move his plan into high gear.

WHEN LILY WALKED into her yard the next day for lunch, Beau was there, sitting in the glider on the front porch drinking lemonade with her mother. God, the man was like a bad penny. He turned up everywhere.

"Lily," her mother said. "We have a guest."

"So I see."

Beau held up his glass. "Great lemonade. Want me to pour you a glass?"

As much as she wanted to snub him, she wanted a glass of her mother's cool, tasty lemonade more. "Thank you." She took the glass he handed her and sat down in a nearby wicker rocking chair.

"Beau was just telling me about his plans for the Friday night party. Did you know there was going to be live music?"

"Yes."

"Uh, what did you say the name of that group was, Beau?"

"Times Past. A combination big band, fifties rock and roll group."

"But he's also hired another group for the young people. Wasn't that thoughtful?"

"Very."

"And the Hyatt in Richmond is catering. Fancy, huh?"

"I want everything to be special," Beau said. "Another reason I won't take no for an answer, Amelia. You have to come."

"Oh, that's really sweet of you, but—"

He held up his hand. "I can be very persuasive when I set my mind to it. Just ask your daughter."

Lily stared as her mother laughed, actually laughed out loud. Persuasive didn't even begin to cover it, she thought. He was calling her Amelia and she was laughing.

"I must admit it does sound like fun. Don't you think so, Lily?"

"What? Oh, yes."

"And I expect you to save a dance for me."

Amelia's eyes went round. "Dance? Oh, I couldn't...I haven't... It's been years since I stepped onto a dance floor."

Lily saw the flush on her mother's cheeks, the smile, and thought how young she looked, how sweet and young and lovely. She'd never really thought of her mother in those terms, but now it was easy to visualize how she must have looked as a girl, starry-eyed and happy. It was almost too poignant to watch.

"There you go. Add that to the list of reasons for you to go to the party. I claim the honor of being the first man to waltz you around the floor."

Amelia blushed. "You know, Lily, once upon a time your decrepit old mother was pretty light on her feet. Why, I remember when your father and I..." She stopped, a look of shock in her eyes that mirrored Lily's. Then the shock faded and a slow, wistful smile spread across her lips. "Your father and I used to dance a lot when we first married. He was very dashing, or at least I thought so. And I was pretty then. We made a handsome couple and we had fun." She looked at her daughter. "I think that's what I missed most when he left—the fun."

Stunned, tears filled Lily's eyes. She'd barely heard her mother mention her father over the years, much less talk about him. The warmth in her voice, the nostalgia, almost broke Lily's heart.

"Oh, but that sort of thing is for you young people," Amelia said, coming back from her reminiscence.

"And for the young at heart. Believe me, Amelia. You qualify," Beau said, deeply moved. "Promise me Friday night."

"We'll see," she said, then dismissed him with a wave of her hand. "Now this sentimental old fool better go get lunch ready. Would you care to join us, Beau?"

"Thanks, but I've got some business matters that need my attention."

"Well, then, I'll say goodbye." She rose from the glider and walked to the front door, then turned back. "You know, Beau, I've never thought death was cause for celebration, but if it weren't for Rowland Stuart's death you would probably never have come back to Rosemont. And I'm very glad you did."

"So am I, Amelia. So am I."

After her mother went inside the house, Lily walked to the door, stared through the screen. In the kitchen Amelia Matthews was humming while she worked. "I—I've never heard her talk about my father. Not like that."

Beau heard the quiver in her voice and had to squelch the urge to take her in his arms and soothe

her the way he might soothe a child waking from a
bad dream. Instead he satisfied himself with merely
putting his hand on her shoulder.

"You come by your strength honestly," he said.
"She's a gutsy lady."

"I don't think I realized just how gutsy until today." She looked up at him. "Thank you."

"Me? I didn't do anything but invite—"

"No. You touched something in her. Some lost
emotion she needed to find again. I'm very grateful."

"Maybe she decided life was too short to live it
from the sidelines. Or maybe she just decided it was
time for a change."

Beau looked into Lily's eyes and wondered if she
was ready for the change he had in mind. "I hate to
bring up business but I need you to drive into Richmond with me. The foundation papers are ready for
signatures and it would go a lot quicker if we went to
the lawyer's office to sign them. Can you get away
this afternoon?"

"Well, I..." She thought about refusing him only
because it put them alone together. Again. But, after
what he'd done for her mother, she would be a petty
person indeed to refuse. "I'm sure I can. Let me
check with my assistant. Are you going home first?"

"Yeah. Call me and I'll swing back and pick you
up."

"How long will we be gone?"

"I've got an appointment with my lawyer for

three-thirty. Maybe an hour to look over the papers and sign them. I won't keep you long." With that he stepped off the porch, jogged to his car and drove away.

"But longer than you think," he said, glancing in his rearview mirror. If the afternoon, and the night, went as he planned he would keep her for a lifetime.

10

"T. J. HOWARD, this is Miss Lily Matthews," Beau said, introducing her to his friend and attorney.

"Well, well, I'm sure glad to meet you." A tall, barrel-chested man with thick red hair stepped from behind a massive mahogany desk to shake her hand. "Beau sings your praises. Tells me you've been the real cornerstone of this restoration project."

"I don't know about that."

"Between you and me, I was glad to see him do something worthwhile with that old barn. Sit down, please."

Over the next hour and twenty minutes T.J. went over every aspect of the foundation's charter, painstakingly explaining details to Lily's satisfaction. The time would have gone quicker, but their conference was disrupted four or five times by phone calls for T.J. He apologized, explaining he was involved in a tricky negation for another client that only he could handle. By the end of the session Lily was tired, her nerves a bit frazzled by the constant interruptions. Finally it was over, all the papers signed and Lily was looking forward to a solitary forty-mile drive home to relax.

"It's later than I anticipated," Beau said when they stepped off the elevator and headed for valet parking. "How about we go across the street to the Hyatt, have a drink and let the traffic die down? And while we're there I can check on the catering for Friday."

A perfectly reasonable request, Lily decided. "All right."

But by the time she had sat through a brief meeting with banquet and catering while Beau finalized details, she felt a headache begin to bloom and her energy level drop. By the time they made it to the bar and Beau ordered himself a scotch and her a club soda it had dropped even more.

"You look a little tired," he commented. "You okay?"

"Fine. But I do need to powder my nose." She glanced around the lobby bar in search of the ladies' rest room. Spying the sign she stood up—a little too fast. Suddenly the room started to spin and the edge of her vision faded to black.

Beau glanced up in time to see her sway. He shot out of his chair and caught her as she crumpled into his arms.

"Lily! Oh, God. Darlin', talk to me." He glanced around, spotted a bellboy. "Call a doctor," he barked.

"No," Lily whispered.

He looked down at her, so relieved to hear her voice he didn't mind that even now she was determined to do everything her way.

She put a hand on his shoulder to steady herself. "No doctor. I'm fine."

"The hell you are."

"It's just that I haven't eaten today—"

Beau said something crude then called off the bellboy and his request for a doctor. "You little idiot," he whispered. Then he scooped her into his arms and carried her out of the bar, past the registration desk and into an elevator.

"Beau, put me down," she demanded, albeit weakly, as several guests turned to stare. "People are looking."

"Let 'em." He jabbed a button and the door whooshed closed.

A moment later he stepped onto the concierge floor with her still in his arms and kept walking until they reached a room. He set her down, whipped a card key from his pocket and opened the door to a suite.

"What we doing here?" she said, when they were inside the room.

He kicked the door closed with his foot. "We're having dinner."

"I'm not having dinner in any hotel suite with you. You're taking me back to Rosemont right this minute."

In three strides Beau crossed the room and deposited her on the sofa. "Let's not go into what I'd like to do with you at this moment. But right now I'm going to feed you."

The idea of food was both welcome and abhorrent. Her stomach roiled and she was sorely afraid she might throw up. "I don't—"

"You don't have any say-so here. I'm calling room service and you are going to sit down and have a hot meal—" His eyes widened in alarm when he saw her slap her hand over her mouth and race for the bathroom. "What the..." The sound he heard answered the question he hadn't had time to ask. "Hang on, darlin'," he told her.

The next thing Lily knew a cold washcloth touched her cheek and a strong hand was holding her head. "That's it, baby. Everything's going to be okay."

After seconds that seemed like hours she was picked up in strong arms and carried to the bed. "Don't move," he instructed after gently laying her down and pulling the bedspread over her.

"I can't," she whispered and closed her eyes.

BEAU SAT ON THE EDGE of the bed literally shaking from head to toe. What had he done? He called himself a thousand times a fool for pushing her. And look what had happened. Because he loved her, couldn't imagine his life without her, he'd set out to convince her to marry him with the same single-minded drive he used in business. He couldn't do this. No matter how much he loved her it was no good this way. But what if he lost her? What if, when he backed away, she turned from him and refused to give him a second chance?

But he'd already taken a big risk to win her back. The decision to have T.J. draw up papers forfeiting his parental rights had been one of the hardest he'd ever had to make. It was a gamble and everything was riding on this roll of the dice—fatherhood and Lily. No, he'd come this far, he couldn't afford to blow it by letting his no-holds-barred approach ruin it. It was time to step back, cross his fingers and pray the love he knew was in her heart would be the final truth.

SHE MUST HAVE SLEPT because the next thing she knew Beau shook her gently. "C'mon, darlin'. You need to sit up and eat something."

When she opened her eyes there was a service cart a few feet from the bed and on it was a bowl of what looked like chicken noodle soup, a baked potato, some rice, vanilla pudding and a basket of dinner rolls. "What's all this?"

"I didn't know what you could keep down so I just ordered a bunch of bland food."

Lily couldn't help but smile. "There's enough starch here for a Chinese laundry." She sniffed and discovered she was ravenous. "The soup smells good."

"You got it." He rolled the cart over as she sat up.

Lily took a spoonful. "Hmm. It's delicious."

Beau all but staggered back and plopped down in a chair. "Thank God. You scared me to death."

"I'm sorry. And before you start lecturing, I really did intend to eat the lunch Mom fixed, but I got busy, then it was time to drive to Richmond, and..." She shrugged. "It wasn't deliberate."

"I know. It's just that you were so pale and..." He shook his head and frowned. "Don't do that again."

"Okay."

"No. Promise me you won't go without food. I mean it, Lily."

She'd never seen him so serious. "I promise."

He sighed and ran his hands through his hair. While she finished the soup she noticed his shirt was partly unbuttoned, his tie was gone and he looked rumpled. She'd never seen him look anything but well put together even when he was wearing jeans and a casual shirt.

"Beau—"

He was out of the chair like a shot. "What? You feel sick again? What do you need?"

Then she realized why he didn't look like himself. He was worried about her. "Nothing."

"You sure?"

"Yes. I..." She started to tell him it was sweet of

him to fret over her, but changed her mind. "I was just going to ask if you were eating."

"No."

She smiled. "I'll share."

For the first time since he'd seen her almost collapse in the lobby, Beau relaxed. He'd never been so scared in his life. For one terrifying second he actually thought she might be dead. He'd known panic and real fear, but nothing, absolutely nothing to compare with the gut-level terror of that moment. The realization that he might have to face life without her made him crazy, desperate and to the bottom of his soul sick with fear. Food? The last thing on his mind was food. He shook his head, content to watch her polish off the soup and the baked potato.

"That was wonderful," she said.

"There's more where that came from." He moved the cart away.

"No, thanks." Then she noticed the clock on the dresser. "Good grief. I need to call my mother and—"

"I took care of that."

"What do you mean you took care of it? What did you tell her?"

"That you got a little dizzy—"

"Beau!"

"And I was afraid it might be a relapse of the flu so I had the hotel doctor look you over. He recommended a hot meal, which I ordered and by that time it was late so I decided you should stay the night."

"You what!"

"I gave her this room number and my room number in case she needed to reach you."

"Your...but I thought this was your room."

He shook his head, a scowl on his face. "I can guess what you thought, but I got a room down the hall. My company keeps this suite year-round for out-of-town executives. See, everything is above-board," he snapped.

"Well, you don't have to get mad about it. I'm sorry I got sick and put you to all this trouble, but—"

"Don't." He turned his back on her. "Don't apologize."

She was on the verge of demanding he turn and look at her when she noticed he was shaking. Those big, broad shoulders were shaking.

"Beau? Beau."

When he did face her, it was her turn to be shocked. And he was the one looking pale.

"Lily, *I'm* the one that needs to apologize. You passed out, for God's sake, and it's all my fault."

"How can you—"

"Ever since you told me about the baby I've pushed you to marry me. I've badgered you. My God, is it any wonder you're stressed out? I'd never forgive myself if anything happened to you." He came to the bed and sat beside her. "I'm so sorry. And I promise you, I'm backing off. The games are over."

"Games?"

"I've tried every way I knew how to maneuver you, tease you. All because I thought I knew what was best."

"You meant well."

"But I was wrong. I wanted you and I was willing to do anything to have you."

"Some women would be flattered by that kind of attention."

"Not you. You're too smart. You've been too smart for me from the beginning." He reached out and brushed a lock of hair from her forehead. "Too smart and too beautiful. My only excuse is that I've never met anyone like you. Smart, sexy, and fearless. Absolutely fearless."

"I don't feel very fearless now," she said, undone by his tenderness.

"My fault—"

She put her finger to his lips. "Shh. I'm fine. Our baby's fine. No more apologies."

"Do you realize that's the first time you've said 'our' baby?"

Lily looked into his eyes and saw herself reflected in their depths. And what she saw was love, truth and joy. Oh, how she loved him, and how tired she was of being brave, or at least acting brave. She didn't want to be a magnolia, admired for its strength. Just once, she wanted to be treated like a delicate flower. In his arms she felt safe, taken care of, even if it wasn't the forever kind of safety. "It is ours. We made him, or her, together."

It was the first sign of any real hope of bringing her around to loving him and accepting his love, and he wasn't about to ruin it. A woman needed to be adored, cherished. She needed hearts and flowers, romance and soft words. She needed to know she was wanted for herself, not just her body. He hadn't done much of that, if any, and it was high time he made it up to her. He knew she loved him, but she had to know, feel it in his touch, absorb it like a flower absorbs sunshine. If she didn't, she could never trust her love, or his.

"Just imagine," he said. "The first time we made love we created another human being."

"Kinda scary, huh?"

"So was that night. You blew my mind."

"Did I?"

Beau grinned. "And how. A man dreams about having a gorgeous woman tell him she wants him then proceeds to demonstrate how much. You were—are—a fantasy."

"Fantasy? I never expected to be a man's fantasy. I like that."

"So did I, at first."

"But?"

"After that first night everything changed. I don't think I realized it at the time, but I was hooked. You were too good to be true and I didn't want to lose you."

Suddenly Lily went very still. "What are you saying?"

A direct question requiring a direct answer. And he'd said no more games. If she needed to hear his answer in order to feel safe, to take that leap of faith and trust, then so be it. "I'm saying that I thought I was only getting a fantasy when I was actually getting my heart's desire."

Her eyes welled up. "Beau—"

Now he put a finger to her lips. "Just listen. I told you I'm done pushing, but just this one last time I'm going to tell you how it is. You got under my skin, Lily. So deep I didn't even realize you were part of me until you turned your back and walked away. Yeah, I badgered you to marry me, but not, as you think, because of the baby. Not entirely anyway. I love you. I've known it for a while, but I didn't know how much until tonight. And I think..." He shook his head. "I know you love me, but it's hard for you to trust that. I understand. And I'll wait. Even if you send me away again, I won't go. Whenever you're ready for my love, I'll be here."

Too moved to speak, she simply reached up, captured his handsome face in her hands and pulled him down for a sweet kiss. A kiss of thanks and promise and love.

"Lily," he whispered, taking her mouth ever so gently.

She responded immediately, her body aching for the kind of pleasure only he could bring. She slipped her arms around his neck, tugging him down to the bed with her.

Kissing her was sheer heaven, but he would deserve to twist in hell if he didn't stop. Slowly, stringing little kisses across her cheek, he backed away. "I don't want your gratitude, and you're too tempting. So I think the best thing for me to do is go to my room before it's too late."

"You don't have to go," she said.

"Yes, I do. If I stay—"

"Stay."

"Are you sure, Lily? Sure you don't feel pushed—"

"Stay," she repeated.

He stayed.

He took her hands in his and tugged until she stood beside the bed. Then he turned her around and unzipped her dress, holding her hand to steady her when she stepped out of it. He turned her to face him and slowly, carefully unhooked her bra, slipping it from her body. "I know I've told you I love your skin, but I could say it a thousand times and it wouldn't convey how much I love it. How soft it is. I dream about touching you."

And so he touched her, worshiped her. His hands skimmed over her torso, lightly touching her narrow ribs, the nip at her waist, her soft flat belly.

Lily sighed, her body shivering, but not from cold. From the fire building within her. Every touch, every stroke of his fingertips stoked the fire higher, hotter. She felt flushed and chilled, weak and strong, all at the same time.

He shed his clothes as quickly as possible, not because he was in a hurry for gratification, but because he was in a hurry to get back to her. To continue showing her how much he loved her. Gently, carefully, he pushed her panties down her slender legs, then bent his head and kissed first one hip then the other. "You taste so good."

He slipped one arm under her knees, the other at her back and lowered her onto the bed. Then he laid down beside her. And began to caress her body from eyelash to ankle. First with his hands. Then with his mouth. He played her body the way a concert violinist might play a Stradivarius. Worshipfully, delicately. And she responded like that finely tuned instrument of pleasure, joyfully giving everything to him, the artist, the creator and caretaker. In his hands it became one measure after another until finally the melody soared, crescendoed into one single exquisite note of pure joy, sensual and spiritual. And as that note sang through her, she proclaimed her love.

MANY HOURS LATER Lily woke to the muffled sound of voices coming from the other room. Bright sunlight peeked through miniblinds, slanting shafts of light across the floor. She got out of bed, found a plush terry-cloth robe provided for the hotel's special guests and slipped into it. She peeked around the door to the parlor side of the suite and found Beau sitting on the sofa, drinking a cup of coffee and talking on a speakerphone.

"I really appreciate you getting those papers in order yesterday."

"No sweat," T.J. told him from the other end of the line. "And how did you like my performance? I expected Lily to get antsy with all of those preplanned interruptions."

"You were fine."

"How did the rest of the evening go?"

"Equally fine. You delayed things just long enough for me to get her to the hotel."

"And how did you talk her into staying the night?"

"I didn't have to."

"You mean you went to all the trouble to finagle her into town, trick her into going to your hotel room and you didn't even have to persuade her to stay."

"Something like that."

T.J. chuckled. "I got to hand it to you, buddy. When you set out to get your lady, the mounted police have nothing on you. Although I must say, this time you got better than you deserve. Lily is one terrific-looking lady."

"No argument there. And I got the other papers this morning by courier. Thanks."

"Oh, the Forfeiture of Rights to the baby and the Disclaimer? All they need is a signature and it's a done deal."

"I may not need them, after all."

"Really? How's that?"

"After last night, I think she may come around on her own."

"You devil. You always did like to have your cake and eat it, too."

Lily backed soundlessly into the bedroom, turned and ran to the bathroom and closed the door. T.J. had deliberately delayed the conference yesterday afternoon so Beau could trick her into going to his hotel room? It didn't make sense. But words like *Forfeiture of Rights* and *Disclaimer* kept buzzing around in her head. The conversation she'd just overhead sounded like...but it couldn't be... Beau couldn't intend for her to forfeit her rights to the baby. He couldn't mean for her to disclaim her own child. He couldn't be that cruel. Could he? He wasn't still trying to manipulate her, was he? Oh, please, not again. She couldn't have been a fool twice for the same man.

Not after pouring out her heart to him last night. Not after telling him how much she loved him.

But he'd damned himself with his own words. She'd heard them herself.

Just like she'd heard him say he loved her. Just like she'd heard him whisper words of endearment while making passionate love to her.

Suddenly the only thing she wanted to hear was the creaking of the glider on her front porch. All she wanted was to be far away from Beau. She snatched up her clothes and quickly got dressed. She was just stepping into her shoes when Beau strolled back into the bedroom.

"Good morning, gorgeous."

Thankfully her back was to him. She didn't want him to see her tears.

When she didn't answer he slipped his arms around her waist and pulled her to him. He nuzzled her neck. "Marry me."

Lily spun around, the pain of betrayal racking her body. "Not if you were the last man on earth." And she ran out of the room.

BEAU DROVE LIKE A BAT out of hell, breaking speed laws right and left, to catch Lily, but couldn't. Fortunately there was only one place for her to run. He didn't know what had gone wrong, but he sure as hell intended to find out.

Lily had been in the house only minutes when she

heard a car screech to a halt in her driveway. It had to be Beau.

"I don't want to see him," she told her mother. "I won't see him."

"Lily, can't you tell me what happened?"

There was a banging on the door. "Not now. Just tell him to go away."

More banging, loud enough for half the neighborhood to hear. "All right, dear. If you're sure?"

"Oh, I've never been more sure of anything in my life."

The pain went so deep, hurt so bad, she couldn't afford to dwell on it or it would consume her. Instead she focused on anger. Pure, hot anger.

More banging, harder. "Lily! Open this door before I break it down. Oh," he said more calmly when Amelia opened the door. "Sorry, but I've got to see your daughter."

"She doesn't want to see you, Beau. And I have to respect her wishes."

"Well, I don't." He yanked the screen door open and plowed past a bewildered Amelia. "There you are," he roared when he found Lily in the living room.

At that moment Pauline came in the back door. "What's all the racket about? I can hear it clear across the alley. Amelia, what's going on?"

Amelia only shrugged her shoulders and looked from Beau to her daughter.

Lily tilted her chin higher and looked him right in the eyes. "The only thing going on, Aunt Pauline, is that Mr. Stuart has finally shown his true colors. That's all."

"What the hell has gotten into you?" Beau demanded.

"Me? Oh, nothing except that you might say I'm a lot wiser than I was an hour ago."

"Lily. I want you to tell me why you stormed out of the hotel room without an explanation, and I want you to tell me right now."

Pauline's eyes widened and she glanced at her sister-in-law. "Hotel room? Did you know about this?"

Amelia only shook her head.

"Leave this house," Lily ordered.

"Not until I get an explanation."

"You don't deserve one."

"The hell I don't. Not an hour ago I asked you to marry me."

Pauline gasped. Amelia remained silent, but watchful.

"And you got your answer."

"And last night? What about last night? You said you loved me."

'That was before I discovered you were a liar. You know, I underestimated you. Last night when you admitted to maneuvering me I thought it was sweet. Little did I know it was just another ploy to get me to hand over my baby to you."

Pauline and Amelia gasped.

When Lily realized what she'd said, tears filled her eyes and she turned to her mother. "I'm... Oh, Mom, I'm so sorry. I didn't mean for you find out like this."

"You should be ashamed of yourself, young lady. I've never been so—"

"Pauline," Amelia warned.

"I'm the father," Beau said, slowly calming himself.

"Oh, my God! We'll never live this down."

Amelia turned to her sister-in-law. "Pauline. Shut up!"

Pauline Jackson's mouth dropped open and she stared in disbelief at the usually mild-mannered woman beside her. "And don't say another word," Amelia said. "This is between Lily and Beau. So, just butt out."

Pauline's mouth snapped shut and she crossed her arms over her chest with a huff. "In fact—" Amelia took her arm "—let's go in the other room." And she led the stunned Pauline into the kitchen.

"Now," Beau said. "Suppose you tell me why you think I've used you in some ploy?"

Calmer now herself, Lily knew it was only a lull. Unless she confronted him with everything she knew, she'd never be free of him. Him and his pit bull determination. "I heard you talking on the phone."

"So? I talk to T.J. every— Oh." He nodded. "I get

it. You put two and two together and came up with five."

"I don't see anything humorous in this situation."

"This situation, as you call it, is of your own making. Why didn't you just ask me about my conversation with T.J.?"

"I didn't need to. It was obvious—"

"Obvious? You know, you're a really smart woman, Lily. It's one of the things I admire most about you."

"Don't think you're going to smooth-talk your way around this."

"But sometimes smart people are too smart for their own good. They know all the answers when they don't even hang around long enough to ask the right questions. Like whether those paper T.J. mentioned were for you or me?"

"I—I don't understand."

"Because you didn't stay to find out."

"What about the 'preplanned interruptions'?"

"T.J. killed time as a favor to me because I wanted to be alone with you and we couldn't do that in Rosemont."

"So you did trick me."

"For the best of reasons."

"And the papers?"

"They were for me to sign. I had them drawn up the day after you told me about the baby. I knew I couldn't force you to love me and I decided that if a piece of paper saying we weren't tied together could make you feel free, then I would do that much if only the baby carried my name."

"Y-you were going to forfeit your rights?" she asked, knowing the emotional price he'd paid in making such a decision.

"If that's what it took to get you to trust me? Yes. And I have the papers right here." He pulled them out of his pocket and held them out to her. "Proof positive, Lily."

He was giving her everything she wanted and on her terms. This wasn't manipulation, it was capitulation. No, more. It was the kind of sacrifice that could only be borne out of love.

"You don't have to trust my word." He took a deep breath and added, "But I won't lie and say that, papers or no papers, I intended to do whatever it took to change your mind, even if it took years. I still do. I—I can't imagine my life without you now. And I don't want to."

She heard the unspoken words in his statement. She didn't have to trust him, but there was no hope for her, or them, if she didn't. He was offering her the opportunity for something real, no matter how it had started. She understood that now.

"And the part about me coming around on my own?"

"I hoped you would come around to accepting my proposal on your own. Because I know you love me,

I know you need me, and God knows I need you. So?"

"So."

He still held out the papers. "This is the last time I'll ask you. Will you let me love you and our baby? Will you marry me?"

He'd spoken the truth for both of them. She didn't want a life without him. "You think you've smooth-talked your way into my heart?"

"Oh, darlin', I sure hope so."

"And you think I'll do whatever you want because I'm in love with you, right?"

"Well..."

"Well?"

"Well...no. If I've learned nothing else, I've learned you can't be pushed."

"That's a step in the right direction." Seeing the flash of desperation and hope in his eyes she didn't have the heart to torture him further. So, she took the next step. And it was definitely in the right direction.

Carefully, so there was no mistaking her answer, Lily took the papers and tore them into shreds. Then she stepped into the arms of the man she loved.

Epilogue

FROM THE DOORWAY of the bedroom Lily watched Beau dress for the street fair. He was so beautiful, his body near perfection, she thought, as he stepped into a pair of well-worn jeans that molded to his hips and legs so seductively her mouth watered. And his shoulders were so broad and strong, it was a shame to cover them with fabric. She sighed as he did just that, slipping on a casual shirt. Not that she advocated him going around naked from the waist up all the time, but the idea did have possibilities.

Possibilities. Her life was filled with them now. Just like Beau filled her heart, her mind...her world.

"You know, you're way too handsome for your own good."

Beau turned, smiling. "Think so?"

"I know so, and so do you. Who are you trying to impress?"

He walked to the door, took her by the hand and drew her inside and into his arms. "You, of course."

"More of your smooth talk."

"You're a smart, beautiful woman and they don't exactly grow on trees you know. So, I figure I need to work at this relationship, keep the romance going.

You know, doing things like sending flowers, telling you that you're as gorgeous as the day I married you. Things like that."

"Beau, we've been married for two days."

"That long."

"Hmm. An old married couple," she told him, loving the word, the man, the promise of years together. She closed the door. "Much too married to do this." She wrapped her arms around his neck and kissed him long, deep and hard. "Or, this." She unbuttoned the first three buttons of his shirt and planted baby kisses on his chest. Her hand slid toward his belt buckle. "Or..."

"Stop right there."

"Problem?"

"There will be if you don't stop. We've got a whole town waiting on us. How would it look to the town and the mayor if the host of this blowout affair showed up noticeably aroused?"

She leaned in for another kiss, but he held her off, albeit reluctantly. "I won't complain."

"That's because you're a shameless hussy who can't keep her hands off her husband."

"True. But I didn't hear you objecting last night, or this morning." She stepped closer and ran her hands up his arms encircling his neck. Then she pressed her body to his.

"Oh, you are shameless, Mrs. Stuart." He had no

defense against her honest passion. Never had. Never would.

"Thank you, Mr. Stuart." Again, she reached for his belt buckle, this time without resistance. "Didn't I hear something a second ago about an arousal?"

"Now, Lily..." He made one last, feeble attempt at reason.

"Now. Beau."

"To hell with the mayor," he growled and kissed her then pulled her toward their bed.

Lily almost had his jeans unzipped when they heard a knock on the door. She stopped.

Beau never missed a beat. She'd gotten him started and he was in no mood to stop. So he went right on kissing her neck, her ear, the wildly beating pulse at the hollow of her throat. Especially the hollow of her throat. So sweet and hot he could feel the need racing through her veins.

"Lily," Amelia said through the closed door.

"Ye—" Beau cupped her breasts and squeezed ever so slightly. "Y-yes, Mother?"

"It's almost time to go, dear."

"We'll be down...in a few minutes...Amelia," Beau told her between kisses.

"Oh, uh...yes, of course."

"Beau," Lily said as her mother's footsteps faded down the long hallway leading to the stairs. "Beau..."

"You started this," he reminded her.

"I know." With a deep sigh of regret, she moved out of his reach as much for herself as anything. "But you were right. We shouldn't keep everyone waiting."

He rolled his eyes. "Now she tells me."

"I'm sorry."

"It's all your fault, you know."

"I apologized. And I'll make it up to you tonight."

"No." He straightened her blouse then held her hand. "I mean all of this. You, me...everything is your doing. If it hadn't been for you and your all-fired determination—" When she opened her mouth to protest he kissed it closed. "I said determination, not stubbornness. If it hadn't been for you, I never would have realized I'd been hiding from my past, and we wouldn't be married and about to attend the biggest fence-mending party in history." He looked into her eyes. "And I wouldn't have more happiness than any man has a right to expect. I love you, Lily. I want to raise this baby." He put a hand on her still flat tummy. "And lots more."

"Oh, Beau." Her eyes filled with tears.

"I know you're worried about what some people may say when our son—"

"Or daughter."

He grinned. "Have it your way." Then he was serious again. "As much as I wish otherwise, I can't stop folks from counting to nine or prevent sidelong glances and—"

"I'm not asking you to, but I love you for wanting to. And you're right. There will always be people to gossip, but they can't touch us now."

"What about your mother and Pauline?"

"It's different now. I've never seen mother so...strong. She's even telling Aunt Pauline what to do. And suggesting that they take over running the museum together was nothing short of brilliant. They'll be so busy they won't even miss me when we move to Richmond." She kissed him gently on the mouth. "You're a magician. Or maybe that's just another name for a good-looking, sexy, smooth-talking charmer."

"The best talking I ever did consisted of four words. Will...you...marry...me?"

"Repeatedly."

"Worked, didn't it?"

"Beautifully."

Beau looked at her and thought how Fate had literally brought her to his doorstep. He'd always been with smart, sexy, savvy women, no strings, no regrets. But all of a sudden this beautiful woman turned the tables on him and changed his life. He'd thought he was only in for a little Southern comfort and look what he got.

Everything.

Back by popular demand are

DEBBIE MACOMBER's

Hard Luck, Alaska, is a town that needs women! And the O'Halloran brothers are just the fellows to fly them in.

Starting in March 2000 this beloved series returns in special 2-in-1 collector's editions:

MAIL-ORDER MARRIAGES, featuring
Brides for Brothers and *The Marriage Risk*
On sale March 2000

FAMILY MEN, featuring
Daddy's Little Helper and *Because of the Baby*
On sale July 2000

THE LAST TWO BACHELORS, featuring
Falling for Him and *Ending in Marriage*
On sale August 2000

Collect and enjoy each MIDNIGHT SONS story!

Available at your favorite retail outlet.

HARLEQUIN®
Makes any time special ™

HARLEQUIN®
Temptation.

COMING NEXT MONTH

#777 HOT-BLOODED HERO Donna Sterling
Sweet Talkin' Guys

Cole Westcott's marriage to fiery redhead Tess McCrary was
supposed to be temporary—and strictly platonic. But Tess
soon found herself dangerously attracted to her hot-blooded
husband. And sweet-talkin' Cole was hard to resist when he
suggested that, since they were living together anyway, they
might as well share a bed....

#778 ALMOST A COWBOY Ruth Jean Dale
Gone to Texas!

It was "women only" week at the Bar-K Dude Ranch, but
Simon Barnett showed up and refused to leave, hollering sexual
discrimination. Owner Toni Keene realized the sexy, self-made
millionaire was used to getting what he wanted, so she let him
stay. Too late, she realized Simon had decided he wanted *her*,
too!

#779 SIMPLY SCANDALOUS Carly Phillips
Blaze

Wealthy Assistant D.A. Logan Montgomery needed to ruin his
reputation! Otherwise, his father would never give up pushing
him into politics. Logan was hoping a very *public* fling with a
woman whose family was steeped in scandal would do the
trick. But once he met gorgeous Catherine Luck, Logan realized
he'd give up everything for one night in Cat's bed....

#780 THE COLORADO KID Vicki Lewis Thompson
Three Cowboys & A Baby

Matty Lang was hopelessly in love with rancher
Sebastian Daniels. So she couldn't believe it when she found
out a *baby* had been left—on *his* doorstep. Worse, Sebastian
thought the little buckaroo was his! There was only one thing
to do—seduce Sebastian absolutely senseless. Because no baby
girl—or her absentee mother—was going to stop Matty from
getting *her* man....